# Choosing Up
# SIDES

# Choosing Up
# SIDES

## JOHN H. RITTER

PHILOMEL BOOKS • NEW YORK

I wish to give thanks for the kind assistance, long-term memories, and pretty-true stories of many good-hearted souls, including the Reverend Edwin C. Gomke and my father, Carl W. Ritter, onetime sportswriter for the *Ashtabula Star Beacon*. And to my editor, Michael Green, who saw more than I dreamed. Also, a special thanks to those rowdy old Buckeye farm boys—my uncles, Paul, George, and Bob, who made me believe I could dot the i.—JHR

Philomel Books, Reg. U.S. Pat. & Tm. Off.
Published simultaneously in Canada.
Printed in the United States. Book design by Gunta Alexander.
The text set in Trump Mediaval.
Library of Congress Cataloging-in-Publication Data.
Ritter, John H., 1951– Choosing Up Sides / John H. Ritter.
p. cm. Summary: In 1921, thirteen year old Luke finds himself torn between accepting his left-handedness or conforming to the belief of his preacher-father that such a condition is evil and must be overcome. [1. Self-acceptance–Fiction 2. Left- and right-handedness–Fiction 3. Fathers and sons–Fiction.] I. Title.
PZ7.R5148Le 1998 [Fic]–dc21 97-39779 CIP AC
ISBN 0-399-23185-4   3 5 7 9 10 8 6 4

*To Cher, with love.*
*And to my mom, for her smile and grace.*

# CHAPTER

# I

I grew up with my left hand tied behind my back. Well, actually, it was only tied up till I was six or seven.

I figured it was all on account of my Uncle Micah, Ma's only brother. He worked as a newspaperman up near Cleveland. He smoked tobacco and had a certain tendency to get drunk. He also had a tendency to go out dancing all night. But worst of all, he tended to smoke his cigars or drink his drinks or write down notes using his left hand. The hand of the Devil, Pa called it. "Pure backwards of what's right and good."

"Leave a boy go left-handed," he once told my ma, "and he'll turn out wild as a witch-dog, same as your fool brother, Micah." Then Pa hitched up close and whispered down at the both of us. "And I ain't about to let that happen."

See, I had that tendency toward being left-handed, too. Couldn't help it. That's just the way I's born.

Back in the early spring of 1921, we were brand new

in town. Crown Falls, Ohio, a little dot on the map that hardly had two cows to rub together. My pa was a preacher and he moved us around a lot. That's how it'd always been, anyhow. Ma said this time was supposed to be different.

The Holy River of John the Baptist Church Council had sent us here. Now that the Great War was over and Prohibition had started up, Pa said those Holy River Baptizers down in Memphis figured it might be a good time to spread the word up north. And Crown Falls, set smack on the Ohio River border with West Virginia, was a fair enough stretch north for them.

They always picked us a river town, too. Reason was, then, like John the Baptist back in the Bible days, you could take and fully dunk a sinner when you saved him.

Me, I didn't specially care where I lived, long's we had the river by. My river. The great Ohio. I'd spend hours roving the craggy cliffs above its rushing narrows or working its woody shoreline for treasure. I didn't care a coal bucket about baptizing. What I cared about was trapping and fishing.

Even so, I'll never forget that morning we first glimpsed our new church and home.

"That's *it*?" my little sister, Chastity, blurted out as the deacon's motor car coughed to a stop.

"Sure is, sweet pie," said the round-faced churchman with the crab-apple nose. "Purty little redbrick House of God, ain't it?"

2

I studied the dirt-stained glass, the hawk's nest spilling from the bell tower, and the tilted white cross.

Ma took a deep breath behind her hand, but she knew her place. She let Pa talk.

Pa's thin hand rubbed the stubble on his bony jaw. "Do just fine, Deacon Booker," he managed to say.

Chastity bit her lower lip and wrinkled her five-year-old nose at me. I patted her knee.

Forget the ugly church, I thought. I was just relieved Pa didn't rant up and explode in some righteous anger.

Wouldn't take much, either. I'd seen it happen with less call than his realizing he'd been sent off to some podunk town to resurrect a fallen-down church.

A little steel rod of a man, Pa was sometimes hesitant to speak out, but you wouldn't want to judge his caution as weakness. He used it more like a wary cat waiting for the right time to pounce.

It's how he'd do. He'd flare up, do his damage, then slink off somewheres. But the next time you clapped eyes on him, he'd come purring up like the pious preacher folks figured him to be.

What he was thinking now, behind his green cat eyes, I could only guess. But I was sure to hear about it later, soon's this sugar-talking deacon had gone chugging down the road.

"And 'round back," Deacon Booker said, pointing along the rutted gravel drive, "sets your place."

We all eyed the dusty, ramshackle two-storied house, the slanted porch covered with creeping brambly vines.

"Well, Luke," Pa said to me. "You got your work cut out."

"Methodists," said the deacon, "been up and gone a few months now, and it does show. But we'll get some men out here. Have that old parsonage clean as a bird whistle in no time."

Parsonage—that's a fancy word for a dirty, drafty, white-washed house full of hand-me-down furniture indoors and tall weeds outdoors. They give it to a preacher's family so they can pay him hardly nothing and have his family handy to work for free.

Up the drive come the stake-bed hay wagon stacked full of our belongings. With the steady crunch of river rock, it rolled up alongside and creaked to a stop.

"Let's get to work," said Pa.

We poured out of Deacon Booker's black Model T and set to unloading, hefting our crates quiet as pallbearers.

During those first few days, after school and after chores, I spent hours walking trails, trying to find the good hunting spots. Sometimes I headed riverside to check the fishing and scout the streambeds for places to set my muskrat traps.

Towards sundown I might hunker in a backwater cove somewheres and skip a pile of stones over the water. And most times I did it with my right arm. I figured the more I used my right arm, the more natural I'd get.

Then one afternoon during that first week, I heard shouting and cheering rise up from over the hillside. After a spell, I set down my weed scythe and followed a deer trace through the thicket just to see what all the caterwauling was about. From the hilltop, I spied a bunch of boys playing baseball.

I'd heard tell of baseball and I knew something about it, but I'd never actually played the game before. Where I come from, we mostly ran with our own kind. Less chance that way to wander off the path. And on my path, baseball wasn't allowed.

See, Pa frowned on sports. The whole church did. To them, competition fed on vanity and pride, so sports was as sinful as dancing or watching moving picture shows. Pa said those kinds of things were nothing but the Devil's playground, which'd only lead a man to drinking or gambling or woman chasing. "Just like your fool Uncle Micah," he liked to say.

But on that day I figured it wouldn't hurt to watch. At thirteen years old, I wasn't much worried about drinking and such. And besides, baseball held a certain mystery for me. Like the apple that Eve gave to Adam, it was forbidden. But I always figured Adam's mistake was rushing in to take the bite. Whereas a wiser man might've judged the fix he was getting into, then tossed the apple back and gone about his business.

So I snuck on down to the flatlands and stood a ways off, behind a boy who was out there all by himself. He was looking the other way, towards the fellows with the ball.

And that's when something happened. And it soon became the plague of me.

I was just watching. Then one tall, skinny kid stood

up with the stick in his hand and they threw the ball at him. He hit it so far, it even flew past that fellow standing in front of me. Clear over his head.

Rolled right up to my feet.

"Throw it in," some boy yelled. "Here, throw it to me."

By then everyone was yelling the same thing. "Throw it. Throw it here. Throw it home."

So I picked up the ball and heaved it as hard as I could. I threw it over everybody. All those players, all that commotion where everybody was running around, I threw it over them all. And I wished I never did.

It was just pure reaction, and I's glad Pa wasn't there to see.

It made a hush come. It was like a giant cloud full of quiet had blown up and smothered every single shout.

They all stopped and looked at me.

"You see that?" I heard one say.

And I knew I'd done wrong. I'd tossed that baseball straighter and farther than any rock I'd ever thrown, and I was so sorry about it. How I's raised, it wasn't allowed.

They all stood pointing and talking—every boy in town—but I just hung there frozen, praying they'd never say a word to Pa.

Bad enough throwing that baseball. But I had used the Devil's arm.

# CHAPTER

# 2

At church that first Sunday, I was on my best behavior.

Pa stared out over the red mahogany pulpit, narrow-eyed, stone-faced, gathering his thoughts, I reckoned, gathering the way clouds built up tall and dark before a storm.

With Ma and Chastity in their Sunday sackcloth dresses and me in my seam-stretched shirt and pants, we looked every bit the shanty-poor preacher's family we were.

We sat in the front row, me and Chas on either side of Ma, our eyes looking straight ahead, careful not to fidget, not to give Pa any good reason to be ashamed of us.

By my cipher, there set just seven other people scattered among the dark oaken pews behind us. And most of them just curious acquaintances Pa had met since we'd arrived.

"Welcome," said Pa. "Welcome, my friends."

And I heard that purring tone of voice he used in order to summon an image of pious reflection. Coaxing, soothing, calm. He would take us all in with that voice, to where we felt good and safe. I loved to hear it. I wished it'd last forever. But I knew what was building.

"The Holy Ghost," Pa started, "led Jesus into the wilderness where he did not eat for forty days. And after his fast, Jesus was hungered. So the Devil came up and he said, 'You're the Son of God. Turn those stones yonder into bread and feed yourself.' But instead, Jesus turned to the Devil and said, 'Man shall not live by bread alone, but by the word of God.' "

No one coughed. No one stirred. Pa smiled and looked us over.

"Then the Devil flew Jesus to the top of a giant mountain and showed him all the kingdoms of the world at once."

Now Pa's voice rose and the sugary coaxing was gone. "And the Devil said, 'I will give you *all* these riches.' " Pa swooped his arm. " 'I will give you *all* this power and *all* this glory, if you will fall down and worship *me*!' "

He sucked in a quick breath and kept going. "And Jesus shouted, 'Get thee be-*hind* me, Satan! For it is written, thou shalt worship the Lord thy God and Him *only*!' " He slammed his hand down on the pulpit, louder than a gunshot.

Pa let the echo wave through the empty church, let

one lady squirm and cough into a hankie, then he softly added, "And Him only."

He looked right at me. How he figured out what I'd been thinking all week, I'll never know. How sneaking over the hill and throwing that baseball kept coming back to me. How some of the boys at school had started in on pestering me about playing ball. And how the fun I saw on that ball field—the shouting and carrying on—how it didn't seem all that evil to me.

But he knew. He knew it all. Someone must've told him something, I figured. Someone in here had told him!

I lowered my eyes. Pa was saying plain and true that it'd been Satan leading me up that mountaintop. That it was Satan who had me pick up that ball and throw it.

I didn't move. Stared straight at my folded hands. I would not let Pa read my face. Or the worry in my brain. But, oh, I felt sorry. Dear God, I felt so sorry.

"Folks," he said. "We have a church to build. And you might be tempted to look around today and see that it's not glorious, that it is indeed humble, that it needs a goodly amount of repair. But I urge you not to be swayed by those thoughts, to put those thoughts behind you, and do as the Apostle Paul taught when he said, 'Press toward the mark.' "

Wait a minute, I thought. He'd changed his whole tune. I listened to the words behind the words and realized Pa wasn't preaching just to me at all. But he'd roped me in—roped us all in, I bet—with that temptation stuff. Made us all feel guilty as sin. I tell you, Pa was *good* at his job. Mighty good.

"We have a church to build," he repeated. "Plenty of hard work to be done, but hard work, friends, is the backbone of the Holy River Baptist church. And, sure, there's temptation to battle—'Should I commit myself or not?'—Devil thoughts to guard against—'Do I have time for this obligation?'—but I'm here to tell you, the call from God is *stronger*! You would not *be here* if it weren't! We have the time, friends, and we have the talent to build a great church. To spread this good word. Let us press on toward that mark. Paul knew he wasn't perfect. God knows, we're none of us perfect. But we press on, friends. We press *on*!"

And he did. On and on, he roared about sin, sin of the flesh, sin of the heart, sin of the lazy man. Roared like a revivalist. Like the Reverend "Horseback Harry" Jubilay come to save any soul within earshot, Pa moved to one side of the pulpit, turned, then slide stepped to the other. His booming voice filled the empty church like lightning to a midnight sky.

And my heart filled with admiration.

Now Pa was rocking in the pulpit, swaying with the song of his words, almost like dancing, dancing to the music of his own words. And his hand come down hard like a drumbeat.

"Like Jesus in the desert," cried Pa, "we must put God first!" He slammed the wood top again. "Like Jesus told the Devil, get out of my way!" Slam. "Don't tempt me, Satan!" Slam. "Don't tempt me to leave this work to someone else. Don't tempt me to not help build this church." Slam. "Don't tempt me to choose the easy way over God's hard work. Don't tempt me to leave this good work to someone else! And don't *tempt me*—" His voice rose up like a swollen river and poured over us all. "—to put any other gods before *Him alone!*"

And on that note he slammed down both hands, eyed each one of us and shouted, "We cannot any of us be perfect. But we are commanded to—" Then he drummed each final word. "—*aim for the MARK!*"

In the silence that followed, I could hear the hawk flutter from the bell tower.

Pa leaned over the pulpit and clung to the front edge with white fingers, then said softly, "Amen."

The entire room let out a breath at once.

Pa bowed his head, gave us a prayer, then pulled out his battered hymnal. He was the greatest, I thought. Truly the greatest. And it only made me feel that much worse for the thoughts I carried that had wedged a new distance between him and me. Between the church and me. Thoughts about playing baseball and the fuss I'd stirred. Thoughts I could not seem to shake.

"We shall forgo the offering today," said Pa, "as my gift to you. Let us close now with a hymn that reminds us to reach out to each other, to all of those in need."

Then he let a slow grin rise. "And maybe next week we'll look about and see a few more souls here among us."

That got us all to laughing a bit and glancing around with quick and nervous eyes.

Ma stood up and walked to the old upright piano.

" 'Throw Out the Lifeline,' " Pa announced. "Someone is slipping away."

Ma pounded out the intro and everyone stood and sang. Sang for pure relief, seemed like. Pure shouting for joy.

After the service, I had to hightail it out of there. I never was all that easy around people. Too much of that first day "how-do" and handshaking could leave a boy like me tongue-tied and sweating, even if I did remember to reach out with the right hand.

Off in the woods I could sort my thoughts. Besides, I had some more scouting to do before I laid my traps out.

I didn't even change clothes. I just snuck out the back, kicked off my shoes, and headed up the trail.

First clearing I come to, I paused to look out over the vast river valley. No matter where I stood, if I could see my river, see the trusty Ohio rolling along, I was home. That river brought iron ore, salt, and coal by the barge load. And it brought me peace.

A rabbit wandered out between a couple mayapple bushes and started nibbling some fresh grass on the edge of the clearing. That got my attention.

Good spot for a rabbit snare, I figured. If I could find the right tree to hitch it to.

Then, just for fun, I walked over and plucked a few mayapples. Throwing had been on my mind for days now, ever since I tossed that ball. And I's feeling so high strung from the service today, I decided to give it a go.

Besides, wasn't any Devil tempting me. I was up here all by myself.

About fifty feet away I spied a huge black walnut tree. I picked me a spot, an old dark hole where a dead branch'd broke.

One by one, I began tossing mayapples.

The first few I threw with my right arm, but no luck. They sailed on past the tree.

So I figured—being alone up here—why not? How *did* one arm measure up against the other one, anyhow? So I gripped the yellow egg-shaped fruit, turning it in my left hand, and decided to find out.

I aimed for the mark.

*Whack!* Dead center.

Every single apple I threw with my left arm hit the target and fell inside. I must've stood there half an hour, plucking and tossing.

Finally, I had to leave. It got to where I felt like someone was watching me. From above.

# CHAPTER

# 3

**H**ey, Luke," a tall, lanky boy whispered to me. "We got us a ball game right after school. How about you coming on down to play?"

It was only my second week in this new school and already trouble was brewing. I knew all about the baseball games these boys played till sunset. Could hear their shouting sometimes all afternoon. But for now, I'd determined not to go back and watch. Thing was, there seemed to be something about my arm—my "good arm," they called it—that set some of them in on pestering me about it.

Every day it was, "Hey, Luke," this and, "Hey, Luke," that.

I had to admit it was a far sight better than having them pick on me, which was the normal welcome I'd get at most new schools.

But what they didn't know was that even if I wanted to, I couldn't play. My church forbid it.

"I got chores," I whispered back.

"Well, after that," the boy said. "Just drop on by."

The teacher, Miss Wilkens, spun around.

"You'll find your assignments on the board," she said. "And I expect quiet while you work on your recitations. Dexter Lappman, that means you."

The tall kid—Dexter—grunted, then motioned to me with his hand as if to say, "We'll talk about it later."

I buried my face in "O Captain! My Captain!" a Walt Whitman poem the whole class had to memorize.

Somehow I had to make Dexter realize I just couldn't do it. But it felt good to be wanted. And the fact was, I did have a knack.

Yesterday on the mountain taught me that.

Pa would've whipped me good if he'd known what I'd done. But, I figured, what Pa didn't know wouldn't hurt him *or* me. Besides, I only did it to find out how far I still had to go to turn right-handed. Plenty far, it seemed.

Dexter leaned over again. Without moving his lips, he said, "After school."

Miss Wilkens glanced up and glared.

I quick ran my finger under the lines of poetry and moved *my* lips big and quiet.

Around me I could hear the shuffle and buzz of twenty-four other seventh and eighth graders. Poor river kids mostly, not the strapping farm boys I knew down south. Clothes patched and thread worn. Some shoeless, some shod.

I didn't mind memorizing—at home I had to learn a

new Bible verse every day—till I read that this poem was about Abraham Lincoln, who'd set all the slaves free. Pa wouldn't like that. He'd be first to tell you Mr. Lincoln was wrong. That in Ephesians it says all slaves should be obediant to their masters. So now, this just became one more thing I'd have to hide.

Not that I was outright contrary, but I had my moments. And I'd found by now, especially with some questions I's beginning to have, the more I kept to myself, the better I got along with Pa.

*O Captain! my Captain! our fearful trip is done,*
*The ship has weather'd every rack, the prize we*
   *sought is won.*

I looked up and scanned the room as I said the lines over and over in my head. Pretty Miss Wilkens, who could move so graceful she'd draw your eyes in before you knew it, sat quietly marking papers at her desk.

As near as I could tell this class had eleven eighth graders, which included Dexter. The rest of us were seventh graders, six boys and eight girls.

And right then, one of those girls was staring at me. Annabeth Quinn.

I quick looked away, like you're supposed to do, pretending I was just drifting my eyes and thinking. Then I snuck a glance back, and there she was, still a-looking.

Now if that didn't beat all. What kind of girl would flat stare at a boy, whether he caught her or not? Especially once he'd caught her.

Well, truth told, she was pleasing enough. Kind of a

milky-skinned girl with red touches on her cheekbones. I liked how her long, dark hair rode back into a thick braid. But there was something unsettling about the questions in her eyes.

After school I headed up the road towards my trail, quick as a dog fixed on a coon whiff. Not that I wanted to run right home, but all this baseball talk kind of had me fretful.

See, there were certain days in life when things just turned, and you knew they'd never be the same again. The day I'd thrown the ball had been a turning day. And I was just trying to avoid another.

"Hey, you, Luke Bledsoe! Wait up." I slowed and glanced back. It was Dexter.

In the school yard, everyone called him "Skinny." Watching him run up the path, I could see why. All elbows and knock-knees, he looked like a windblown stick doll.

"Hey," he said, catching his breath. "What're you running for?"

"I got chores, Dexter. My pa—"

"Call me, 'Skinny,' will you? Only my ma and ol' lady Wilkens say 'Dexter.' "

"Okay, Skinny, but I told you, I got no time for going out ball playing. We got a porch needs fixing and the churchyard's full of weeds up to my eyeballs—"

"Weeds! You're talking about weeds? Luke, where the heck'd you come from?"

"Down towards Louisville," I answered. "Before that, Paducah."

"Well," he said, "I don't know how they do down in Kentucky, but this is *Ohio*. This here's baseball country. These parts, baseball's *religion*."

"I never heard such a thing."

"I sure hope to tell ya. Folks here'll come out after a hard day's work, in need of a little reviving, and, boy, we give it to 'em. Even scrimmaging. They just want to come out and hoot and holler and make predictions."

"Predictions? On the game?"

"No, on the whole season. All the games coming up. That caught on last year when we done so good, county champs and all. And see, we got almost every single player coming back this year. Folks're excited. They're starting early, too, expecting us to put on a pretty good show even with our practice games."

"So how's it that I figure into all this?"

He didn't answer right off, just eyed me a second. "Well, that comes down to one simple question. See, nobody around here's ever seen a kid throw a ball like you can. And if there's any chance—listen, can you pitch?"

"Pitch? You mean hay?"

"No." He gave my shoulder a little push. "Baseball. *Pitching*. You ever pitch?"

I shook my head.

"Dang." He blew over his teeth like whistling. "You got one fine arm, you know that?"

"Fine enough, I suppose."

A couple other boys walked up, but Skinny waved them off.

I continued. "But throwing that ball—that was pure accident." I turned and started towards the trail through the woods, hoping to stay ahead of the others walking home.

He kept in stride. "Nobody rifles a ball three hundred and fifty feet on accident. And like I said, last year our team was all-county champs, but this year we aim to be all-state. And right now, all's we're doing is choosing up sides and scrimmaging. But our season starts in a little over three weeks. And we could really use a player like you. You'd make one *hell* of a pitcher, Luke Bledsoe."

I winced at the swear word, fearing a girl might hear. But what he'd said was true. That's where the power of that arm come from—right where the Devil lurked—and I wasn't about to let it loose.

"Not interested," I said. Since Skinny was older than me, I wanted to sound my most definite. "Not a chance on earth."

"Why the *hell* not?"

"Hey," I practically shouted. "You can talk to me or you can swear, but you can't do both."

That set him back some. "Oh, I forgot. You a preacher's boy."

I knew that was coming. Every time some kid looked at me, he was thinking goody-goody. That maybe I wasn't a fighter. Just some preacher's boy who don't cuss and such.

"That ain't it. Look here, I got traps to check, rabbits to gut, work to do. I can't loll and gag like this."

"Well, I got chores, too, Luke. Don't think I don't. But chores get done when chores get done. I'm a man who puts first things first."

A man? I thought. Him? That rankled me. "A man don't put off his work to go play a game, Dexter."

He shot me a hard glare. "He does if the whole rest of his life depends on it." Then he pointed his finger. "Look here, Luke. I plan to be a major league ballplayer some day. And going to the state finals would really help. Now you might could help us get there, or you might couldn't. But there's about ten guys've been yapping at me like a pack of hungry hounds to go see if I can't at least talk you into trying out for the team. Now, shoot, how could just doing that hurt?"

"All them guys come badgering you?" I slowed my step.

Skinny nodded. "And a girl, too. Annabeth Quinn." He gave me a quick look in the eye, then glanced away. "Folks can recognize what you got, Luke. There's a buzz around town. And being lefty and all—" He shook his head. "Shame if you ain't gonna make the best of it."

We reached the hillside trail, which headed towards the forest. I stopped and squared my shoulders at him.

"Well," I said, "you can go tell all of them, Luke Bledsoe's got *two* good arms. And he don't hold that pitching baseball's a good use for either one."

Skinny stayed put while I started up the hill.

After a moment he called to me. "Suit yourself, Luke.

But I say you're wasting a talent. And I mean a God-given talent."

Had to admit, him saying that set off a doubt in me again. Rising up like a slow fire. If God was always right, like the Good Book held, then why'd he go and make me so wrong?

That's when I heard a girl's voice. Annabeth.

She come hustling up towards Skinny, bouncing and grinning. I knew she went home along my same path, but I'd always been far ahead of her.

On the forest's edge, I snapped an elderberry twig and ran my hand over the leaves, pausing a minute, hoping to hear what she had to say.

As Skinny faced the wide, full-toothed smile of this frisky girl, something kicked up inside my chest. The feeling come strange and new. Almost as if I wished she'd come here just to talk to me. The feeling come even more so, once I saw the syrupy look she gave him.

"You're going the wrong way, aren't you, Skinny?" she called out.

He lifted both hands high. "You sure got that right."

She glanced towards me. I turned and started off again. But slower now, listening.

"You coming to the game today?" Skinny asked her.

"Silly question," she answered. "Course I will. You know about me and baseball." Her voice rose up like a singer in the choir. "I *love* baseball."

I knew it right then. Not Skinny, not ten other guys, not even the whole dang town itself could've tempted me to reconsider my decision the way her three words did right then.

I hustled on home. I had to. I knew if I stuck around any longer, things'd only get worse.

And that, just like the thrill of throwing those mayapples with my left hand—so perfect, hard and true—was one more thing I'd have to hide from Pa.

# CHAPTER

# 4

$C$an I help?"

Chastity swung upside down on the porch rail. Her blonde braids swept the deck boards I was aiming to mend.

"You can help most," I said, "by getting out of my way."

She puffed her cheeks out like a pouting chipmunk. "I will if you be nice to me."

That kid could sure nettle you, but she got her feelings hurt easy if you yelled at her.

"Okay, okay. Look, Chassy Bird, I'll tell you a riddle. Just one. Then you skedaddle, you hear?"

"Oh, goody!" She loved the riddles I made up for her.

"Okay, here goes. Tell me, who lives high on a hill and deep underground at the same time?"

She had to come off the rail and stand upright to think. Her face scrunched into a squinty-eyed mask. Finally she said, "The fallen angels?"

"No, not the fallen angels." Now, what kind of a guess was that for a little girl? I wondered.

She thought another moment. "I don't know. I give up."

"Remember what we did yesterday?"

She shook her head slow. Chastity was lucky to remember five minutes ago.

"I give up, Luke. Tell me."

"Ants in an anthill. Remember the anthill we found on the cliffs above the river? And that game I taught you?"

She nodded as the fog in her brain seemed to lift. "Oh, yeah! Can we play that now? Can we play follow-an-ant-for-an-hour like we did yesterday?"

"No, no, Chas. Not now." Though I'd admit, it was fun. You'd be amazed at all the things one single ant does in an hour. "I got chores to do. And you do, too, don't you?"

"I don't have any chores."

Ma pushed the screen door open. "Chastity, come here, honey. I got a rhubarb pie needs crisscrossing, and you're the best crisscrosser I know." She gave me a wink.

Ma had an instinct for judging just how much Chastity I could take. For a slight, deer-legged woman, Ma sure carried a mountain of patience. She could tolerate the rascal in most any kid even better than a kid could. And a far sight better than Pa.

She closed the screen door gentle behind them. I went to prying up the deck.

I'd lied to Skinny about the traps. I hated to, but I had to think of something fast. It was okay, though. I'd pray about it that night.

I hadn't set any traps, yet. But I aimed to, first chance I got. And not just rabbit snares. I also had about fifty steel-jawed muskrat traps to set along the streambeds.

After pounding on the porch a while, I finally shored up and tacked down the worst of it. There was termite lumber we'd have to replace someday. But not today. A few more whacks and I'd be done.

"Is that the way I taught you to use a hammer?"

Pa stood on the ground behind me. I hadn't heard him come.

And I hadn't noticed what he'd seen right away. In my hurry to finish, I was hammering with my left hand. I quick switched back.

"Just wrapping up, Pa." I pounded loud and hard. "That should do it."

"Among the left-handers," Pa started, in a speech I'd heard a hundred times before, "we find the heathen, the lunatic, the criminal-minded. The left side has always been the side of Satan, contrary to God."

I hunched on my knees and waited, prepared for a good long preaching-to.

"On the Judgment Day, Luke, what will Jesus say to those on his right hand?"

" 'Come ye blessed,' " I recited. " 'Inherit my kingdom.' "

"And when he turns to those on the left side, what will he say?"

" 'Depart from me, ye cursed, into everlasting fire, prepared for the Devil.' "

Pa folded his arms across his chest. "I can't follow you every minute of your life, boy. But God does. And the Devil does, too." He leaned close and pinched the back of my neck between his fingers.

Then he whispered. Whenever Pa wanted to make a strong point, he'd never scream or shout. He'd whisper.

"I don't ever want to catch you going left-handed again, you hear? You ain't stupid, are you, boy?"

"No, sir," I whispered back.

He shoved my neck and strode into the house. I heard him slam the door to his study.

No, I wasn't stupid, that's for sure. But I's beginning to think some of Pa's rules were.

# CHAPTER

# 5

Ma always said I took after her brother, Micah. I didn't much look like my Uncle Micah, but she didn't mean that.

Back when I's a little tyke, young as Chastity, I slid down a stairwell bannister, slipped, and crashed into a flower vase and near broke my neck.

"I *warned* you about that," Ma said.

Well, no, not exactly. She'd warned me at the house before that one. I figured a new rail gave me a new start.

"You got a rebel streak in you," she told me, as her hand come down with a slap, "straight from your Grandpa Barnes. Your Uncle Micah has it, and it causes him no end of trouble. And it'll daunt you, too, young man, until you learn to walk the straight and narrow."

I always remembered that day. Maybe that's when I first learned that thinking for yourself was a sin. God had given us fathers and mothers and the Ten Commandments. Every thought you ever had to think had already been thought a long time ago.

Of course, the thing I liked most about Uncle Micah was the fact that he *was* a thinker. And seeing that trait in me, I supposed, was what worried my folks as much as anything.

So, in light of what all I'd been up to lately, I decided I'd best walk a little straight-and-narrower. Just to be on the safe side.

And I started off just fine, too.

That afternoon, once I finished the deck work, I traded my hammer for a hatchet and grabbed a few other things and headed up the hillside to commence working on my rabbit snares.

The sky showed fairly two hours of daylight left. And even though I had work to do on the mountain, I'd snatched my poem book from my room and tucked it under my belt.

Sometimes heading up a hill, I'd take the Bible along. But I already had my daily word memorized. So this time I grabbed Walt Whitman.

I scrambled through the raspberry bushes and kept a lynx eye out for poison ivy. The other day I'd scouted out several good trapping spots, including a perfect silver maple sapling growing near a tall red oak and a cluster of white-flowered dogwoods. It stood right beside a rabbit trail full of fresh droppings. Make a fine tree for a rabbit snare.

The whole secret of setting a good snare trap was

picking the right tree. Couldn't be too big or too small. A two-inch-thick sapling with plenty of spring was perfect.

Once I located the sapling, I tested it again, hitching ahold about seven feet up and bending it down to the ground. Then I let go and watched it snap upright. Perfect.

I chopped the limbs off the maple sapling, then I set a narrow pathway with twigs that would guide the rabbit right through a jute-twine noose and towards a juicy apple.

For bait I'd use one of the Baldwin apples buried under straw near the woodshed. One thing about being a poor preacher's family is that church folks were always bringing by fruits and vegetables and such. I always had plenty of bait for my traps.

The hardest part was rigging the jute loop, since I tended to foul up when I worked line with my right hand. But with no one here to judge me, I quick did it with my left hand.

After rigging the twine, I bent the tree over, dangling the noose off the top of it just so. I anchored the tree tip to a wooden stake set with a trigger—a thick twig stuck through the apple and the stake both. One chomp on the apple would loosen the twig. Then the tree would pull free from the stake, snapping straight up, yanking the noose and the rabbit with it.

Pa said it killed the critter instantly. Broke its neck. I didn't know, I never watched. All I ever found was a dead bunny hanging from a tree. And we had meat for dinner.

Farther up the ridge crest I spotted an old log lying in a bare spot just above a cliff. Now this place, I decided, was just for me. A dandy little hideaway hole to sit and read and sort my thoughts.

All I needed now would be one of them fancy show-boats rolling up the river, pipe organ music rising up to the clouds.

Down in Kentucky, I remembered seeing those tall, bright, majestic boats floating by like shiny pearls. Me and Uncle Micah, with our bamboo poles angling from the bank, would sit and watch their royal parade.

"Hey-ho, you River Dawg!" Uncle Micah would holler, standing and waving his cap. Then one of the showboat pilots, "River Dawg" Dawkins, would blow his whistle at us.

But what I really wished was that I could just walk on board one of them—just once—and lean over her ramparts and ride the river in high style.

Used to see them come by two or three times a month, but ever since the big freeze of 1918, when huge ice chunks busted up all the riverboats, I hadn't seen a single slick-painted paddle wheeler come frolicking up the Ohio.

Pa said those boats were sinful, full of gamblers and show folk, but I loved hearing that music. Could almost hear it now.

I sat down and opened up my book.

*O Captain! my Captain! Rise up and hear the*
  *bells.*
*Rise up—for you the flag is flung—for you the*
  *bugle trills.*

I sat a moment, rolling the sounds off my tongue, over and over again. I could see Mr. Whitman's boat, a ghost ship, with Mr. Lincoln lying on the deck. *Fallen cold and dead.*

Then I heard a great yell rise up from over in the valley. Clapping and cheering. I stood. The baseball game.

I guess that was when my rebel streak come out.

No, it was more than that. It had to do with this whole peck of wondering I'd been up to lately. For instance, what *was* it that all the boys saw in playing baseball, anyhow? And what if, like Skinny said, I *was* wasting a God-given talent for it? Ain't *that* a sin? And so what if I thought about a girl every once in a while? Was that such a sin? Was everything Pa said gospel? But most of all, what was it about baseball that could draw in a girl like Annabeth to come watch?

Couldn't hurt, I figured, to go have another look-see. I wouldn't pick the ball up this time or anything like that. After all, I ain't stupid.

I'd just go and try and understand the game some.

If Pa could quote Scripture for his purposes, then I could, too. The Good Book says, "Get wisdom, get understanding: forget it not."

How could it hurt?

But when I come down off the mountain that afternoon and headed towards the baseball game, I felt more like Uncle Micah or Grandpa Barnes. More like a thinking man than any of my pa's straight-and-narrow-walking Bledsoes.

I sauntered towards the wild crowd gathered on a cluster of green benches. Careful to stay off to one side, I ranged close enough to where I could see it all.

Old men and little boys cheered, standing up and hollering. Some waved their hats. And on the field, it was helter-skelter.

"Send him home! Send him home!" folks yelled.

They focused their eyes on one particular boy.

Skinny Lappman.

He come running towards a dusty canvas bag, stepped on it, then turned the corner and kept on going.

Someone threw the ball right at him and someone else caught it, while Skinny ran, head bent for leather, and skidded down in a pile of dust and dirt.

"Safe!" a fellow called, and he spread his arms wide.

That must've been about the best thing in the whole wide world Skinny could've done because those people went hog wild. Whistling and shouting and stomping their feet.

Then I saw her. And I had to admit, she was the real reason why I'd come.

Amid all that commotion, jumping up and down among all those fellows, was Annabeth Quinn. She clapped and carried on like the rest, shouting and laughing. And I mean pure toss-your-head-back laughter. In all my days, I'd never seen a girl act with such carefree abandon.

I couldn't take my eyes off her. And wouldn't you know, while I's staring like a fool, she turned sideways and looked right at me.

In that instant, it seemed as if I'd been led down a stick-lined path straight towards some sweet apple, only to get my head snapped up so quick it broke my neck.

Like a dead bunny, I hung there with my mouth open.

# CHAPTER

# 6

Annabeth climbed down off the seat boards and hurried my way.

"Wasn't that wonderful?" she asked. "Isn't he just the most exciting ballplayer you ever did see? I tell you, he's heading for the major leagues someday."

"Well, I suppose—" I started, but how could I say? I hardly knew this game. I hardly knew this girl. How could I even talk?

Annabeth stood tall, grinning at me. That was one thing I'd noticed about her. She was bold and nervy. She carried her shoulders back, different from other girls who tended to shy up and slouch a bit around boys.

Annabeth was no slouch.

"Did you come to watch or to play?" she asked.

"Me? No, not to play. I—"

"Oh, that's right," she said. "*Hoo-ly* River Baptizers. Keep to yourselves, don't you? No smoking, no dancing, no moving picture shows, and no sports." She reached up like she was going to touch my arm. "So what *do* you do, anyhow?"

I backed away. "Work, mostly." My ears turned hot as fire. I tipped my cap and stepped to leave.

She followed.

"Wait a minute." Then she called a little louder. "Please, wait a minute. Luke Bledsoe, you're a strange boy, did you know that?"

I kept on going, afraid the more I stuck around, the more I'd prove her point.

She come dogging my heels. "I don't mean that unkindly," she said. "Fact, I admire that. I could tell from your first few days at school you were different."

I slowed a bit. "Like how?"

"Like how you sat so polite. Not squirming, not looking around and making rude sounds like most boys do. You were actually studying the lesson."

I shrugged.

"But, Luke, can I ask you something?"

My stomach tightened. "Go ahead."

"Seems to me," she started, "the way I saw you throw that baseball, you're surely left-handed. But I've been watching you in school. You never use anything but your right hand. Why's that?"

"How I's taught, I suppose."

I hustled on. If Pa'd ever seen me walking with a girl when I should've been out working, he'd probably get down the leather belt.

"So you *are* left-handed." She tried to catch up. "But

what, then? Your folks make you go right-handed? Your church believes that, too?"

I just shrugged.

She stepped abreast. "Well, that's as silly as a saddle on a cow."

There was a time, maybe just a few months ago, that I would've rebuked her instantly, using Pa's words. "If being the Right Hand of God is good enough for Jesus," he'd tell me, "then it's good enough for you." But of recent, some of my own thoughts'd been drifting the same way as hers.

"You wouldn't understand," was all I could manage.

"You're right," she said. "I sure wouldn't. Because that makes no kind of sense to me."

For a while we walked side by side, silent, and I supposed she was thinking, but the trail had narrow spots, which caused her to brush up against me. And each brush with her sent a jolt of weakness through my legs.

Finally she said, "You know what puzzles me even more?"

"What's that?"

"How on earth you do it. If I tried going pure *left*-handed, with writing and such, I'd be miserable."

"You can do anything you want once you set your mind to it," I said. "Specially if it's the right thing to do."

"Luke, hold on, will you?" We bumped at a narrow spot, and that jolt made me stop.

"I swear," she said. "Feels like I'm trotting alongside a Kentucky racehorse."

She stood silent for a moment, staring, pinning me

down with the eyes of a hunter reading a rustling in the brush.

"Will you tell me something?" She leaned closer. "Do you like poetry?"

"*Poetry*?" And she called *me* strange! I blew out a big breath and turned away.

"I'm just curious."

I shrugged. "Yeah, well, some, I suppose." I figured all them Psalms and Proverbs I learned back before I could read had whittled my brain for poetry.

"I thought so."

"Why do you say that?" I asked.

"Can't really say at all. I mean, in words. I just had me a hunch." She bit her bottom lip. "That's how I do sometimes. I get hunches. And I follow them."

Now it was my turn to act puzzled and grin. "So that's what I am? A hunch?"

Her mouth opened like I'd guessed a secret.

"Well, yes," she said, and smiled right back. "Matter of fact. Like yesterday, on my way home from church. Soon as I stepped on the trail, I clapped sight of you running off woods bound in your Sunday best."

She studied me for a response, but I gave her none.

"Well," she continued, "I would've just passed on by. But before I got too far, I started hearing these strange thunking sounds in the woods. So on a hunch, I hiked up a ways. And I saw you standing in a clearing throwing mayapples. Bull's eye, bull's eye, bull's eye. And fast! Luke, I hope to tell ya, you have an arm some men would die to have."

"You were watching me? You were up there?"

She nodded. "And it was like poetry."

I spun on one toe and looked off. "*Poetry*?"

My face heated up again as I realized I'd been spied on. "That's the craziest, most fool dang thing—Annabeth, I know what poetry is. And that was *spying*." I glared at her, but couldn't help putting a tease in my voice. "That how y'all do 'round here? Sit back and spy on people?"

"Oh, no, Luke. I never intended any such thing. I just happened to come along—"

I held up a hand to stop her. "Okay, okay. Lookit, Annabeth." I blew out a breath. "I'm late as it is. I gotta—"

"I know, I know. You have work to do. Fine. I said my piece." Then she shook a finger at me. "But I'll tell you something, Luke. I got a hunch about you—that you're gonna be a great ballplayer someday—and I'd like to see it come true."

I couldn't believe I was hearing this—from a girl who knew the game.

"Well, it won't," I said. "And I don't see why you give a big ding-dang if it does or not."

Her mouth opened wide. I'd tried to josh her, but it'd come out cold and blunt.

"Well," she said, collecting herself. "I'll tell you why, Luke Bledsoe. Because I can throw a baseball, I'll have you know. Not as well as you, but well enough. I can hit one, too. And I'm a good runner and I can catch. I can do practically everything most boys can do, except one. I can't *play* baseball. There's no team for me. And so when I look at you and the opportunity you have, and I see that the only reason you won't play this magnificent game is because of some silly ol' holier-than-thou belief—Luke, it breaks my heart. And *that's* why I give a big *ding-dang*. And I'm sorry I ever brought it up!"

She turned, stumbled over the lip of the trail, then caught herself in two steps, gave a grunt, and stomped away.

Stomped away sorry and mad, I reckoned. Sorry she'd ever brought the whole thing up.

Well, maybe so. But, Lord of Mercy, nowhere near as sorry as me.

# CHAPTER

# 7

In the middle of the night a horn blast woke me up.

"What in thunder?" Pa's voice rang from his bedroom.

One loud knock on our front door and it opened.

"I got a tin can full of night crawlers, and I've been crawling all night!" the man's voice boomed. "You hear? Catfish are calling, and I'm river bottom bound."

Uncle Micah. That big, blasting Gatling-gun voice could send a chill and a thrill through you at the same time.

I rolled out into the black morning and pulled on my dungarees.

Ma ran downstairs a few steps ahead of me, pulling tight her robe and holding high a lamp.

"Micah Barnes," she whispered loud and strong, "you woke the house, the town, and all their kin in the cemetery, too. Have you no shame?"

"Not near enough, thank you kindly." He stood and grinned.

Uncle Micah was a walrus, huge and round with a bushy black mustache hanging down. Moved like a walrus, too. Hulked around, hawing and laughing, chewing on a burnt cigar.

He opened his massive arms. "Come here, sister Ruth. I traveled day and night and broke down twice just to see your clear blue eyes."

Ma could not muster any more anger, though she gave it one last try. She floated towards the old sea creature, saying, "I'll thank you to take that tobacco stick out of my house."

He waved his cigar. "It ain't lit." He stuck it in his pocket. "I don't smoke 'em, anyhow. I just chew 'em down."

I come and stood near the oak hat tree, watching him lift Ma up and squeeze her till she near broke in two.

I knew Chastity was upstairs hiding someplace. I could hear her giggle.

That's when I noticed Pa halfway down the stairs. Dressed in dark suit pants with leather suspenders strapped over an undershirt, he seemed in no hurry to greet his wild and woolly brother-in-law.

Uncle Micah set Ma down. "Zeke," he called.

"Micah," Pa answered with no enthusiasm. "What brings you to these parts?"

"Well, some good old Ohio River catfish for one. Believe I can hear 'em jumping now." He shot me a quick wink.

I loved Uncle Micah. He's who taught me how to fish and how to row a boat. I got all my tackle from him. Where Pa was a woodsy type, Uncle Micah lived for the water.

Pa gave a deep sigh. "I believe, Micah, that a bullhead would be more your style."

Another giggle from the dark.

Uncle Micah roared. "You ain't wrong about that," he said, spinning back to hug Ma again and catch her laugh. "But the real reason I come, I must confess, is business. I'm down here to cover a story." He turned to Pa. "Apologize for arriving in the middle of the night, Zeke. Planned to be here sooner. Brand new Model A Duzy still bucking like a colt."

A brand new Duesenberg Model A car? That was just like Uncle Micah. It probably had all the spangles and jangles and doo-wah-zaree. I wanted to run right outside and climb aboard.

"Paper sent you all the way from Cleveland," said Pa, "for some kind of story?"

Uncle Micah started peeling off his black city-slicker's overcoat. "Not exactly Cleveland," he said. "I quit the *Plain Dealer*. I'm working out of Ashtabula now. Smaller paper, but a bigger job. I'm the new sports editor for the *Star Beacon*."

Pa pounced like a lynx on that. "*Sports* editor?"

I knew what he was thinking.

So did Uncle Micah. "That's right. Most important department in the whole paper, and I run it. I even got a man working under me."

"Well, I swan," said Ma, biting her lip. "Sounds mighty impressive. Micah, let me put some coffee on for you."

Pa started back up the stairs. "Might as well," he said. "Be daybreak soon." I heard his door shut.

"Hey, Trooper." Uncle Micah had called me that ever since he got back from the Great World War. I smiled and approached him. "I wasn't joking about those worms. I got a can full of fat, juicy crawlers and I aim to drown 'em all."

You couldn't wipe the dumb cluck of a tooth-tall grin from my face.

"Okay," I said, before my mind just blanked as this great man stood there, big as all Ohio, and beamed a bonfire of attention at me.

He grabbed a hunk of my hair and shook my head. "Me and you, son. Hit the river at daybreak. You still got the rowboat we built?"

I nodded. "Towed it up when we moved."

"Then let's go!"

I looked towards the kitchen. Ma was kindling a fire in the stove.

"Micah," she called, "he's got school. Plenty time to go fishing after school."

He let go of my hair, but I stood close, letting his big hands knead my shoulder bones.

"School, is it?" he cried. "Well, tomorrow, then, Trooper. They don't hold school on Saturdays, do they?"

"No, sir."

"All right, then. First dawn. How about it?"

"Yes, sir. I'd like that."

"Good. Besides, after I rest up, I plan to spend the day barreling all over the county anyhow."

"Sir?"

"For my story, son."

I'd nearly forgotten he hadn't come all this way just to go fishing with me. "Story about what?"

"Baseball, Trooper. Spring roundup piece on all the best local teams in the state. Supposed to be some young phenom out in these parts who can hit the ball a treetop mile. Tall, thin willow of a lad. Name of Lappman. You might even know the boy. Dexter Lappman?"

# CHAPTER
# 8

I had no idea that Skinny Lappman was fifteen years old or that he was such a great baseball player he was known all over the state.

After Uncle Micah showed up with the principal to take Skinny out of class, the whole school was buzzing.

Now I knew that the book of Proverbs calls envy "the rottenness of the bones." And last thing I wanted was my bones to go rotten. But when I saw Skinny pause at the door to take one quick look back at Annabeth, Lord of Mercy, I did envy him that.

And when I saw her tilt forward and grin and give him a secret wink, I'd never wanted to trade places with someone so much in all my days. Could it be that a sports hero had that much effect on a girl?

That night, suppertime was more quiet than usual, and it's usually quiet enough. Uncle Micah was out racing around in his new red Duzy, calling on some boys in another town.

I had nothing to say I wanted to say out loud. Pa seemed in his usual mood when Uncle Micah was around, downcast and distracted, shoveling mashed potatoes over his chicken and eating it all at once.

At one point he stopped and looked me in the eye. "Do you have your daily verse ready?"

That's how he asked when he wanted me to recite the Bible verse I'd memorized for that day.

And then it hit me. I hadn't *learned* one that day on account of all the fuss and bustle caused by Uncle Micah.

I cleared my throat and pretended to swallow food, trying to buy more time. Could I substitute an old verse—something I'd learned last year? The first one that bubbled up was one that always bubbled up at a time like this. "If a man have a stubborn son, which will not obey . . . all the men of his city shall stone him with stones, that he die."

I couldn't do it. I looked up like a trapped skunk.

"Surely you have something for me," Pa said. "Surely you did not squander the gift of an extra hour this morning. Perhaps you have two. An extra long verse, seeing as how you rose at such an inspirational hour." He sent me a twisted grin, the way a cat might smile at a rat.

"Well, sir. The fact is—"

"The fact is *what*?" His voice rose in anger. "Are you here to tell your father the facts? Are you here to tell your father something he doesn't already know? Is that it?"

"No, sir, I—"

"You *what?* I have no time nor patience for back talk or alibis. I asked you a direct question. Have you a verse ready? I expect a direct answer."

"Yes, sir." My breath come choppy and short.

I could tell he was so all-fired sure I didn't have one, that I decided—stones or no stones—I'd up and give him the one and only verse that sprung to mind.

I set my fork and knife against the edge of my plate. I stiffened up in my chair and looked straight ahead.

" 'O Captain! my captain! Rise up and hear the bells. Rise up—for you the flag is flung—for you the bugle trills.' "

He slammed his hand on the tabletop. Ma jumped. Chastity pitched backward, blinking wildly over an open mouth of food.

Pa could hardly speak. His face turned white and rigid. "I asked for *Scripture*, not some clack and drivel."

No, he hadn't. He'd said *verse.* But I hunched up anyhow and froze.

Pa pushed himself up from his chair.

"Ezekiel—" Ma started, more as a warning to me, I figured, than anything.

He ignored her and strode towards me. "You dare to mock your father, to mock your own father at his table?"

I didn't see the swing coming. He caught me as I sat studying the grease pools in my chicken gravy.

The blow to my ear knocked me clean off my chair. And he wasn't done yet.

"Thou shalt fear the Lord thy God! Him alone shalt thou serve, and to Him shalt thou cleave, and swear by His name."

He ranted on like that for quite a while, but I heard none of it. I sat there on the cold kitchen floor and I buried down inside myself.

Imagine substituting Walt Whitman for Scriptures. What was I thinking? Sometimes when I did things like that, I'd feel like a pure heathen—a nonbeliever of the worse sort.

Thinking. That's what'd done it. What I'd been *thinking*. Thoughts about Annabeth, thoughts about learning baseball and playing for pride and glory.

Pa kept a-raging.

"That man," he said to Ma. "That brother of yours. He's got an influence over this boy."

"How can you say that?" she asked.

"You know what I'm talking about. There's a sinister influence afloat in this house when he comes charging in here all glassy-eyed and moonshined-up. And I won't abide it. And I surely won't abide you questioning *me*."

She drew in a sharp breath, but held her tongue.

I couldn't watch.

Pa lowered down, placing his nose next to my burning ear. "Look at me, boy."

I turned.

He spoke softer now, whispering. "An unholy influence can enter your life, son. It can snake its way into your very soul. It will find your weakest spot and work its way in. It will not rest until it has driven you away from the better angels of your nature. Do you hear me, son?"

"Yes, sir." I stared at my left hand. I knew exactly what my weakest spot was.

"You're at an age, boy, an age when temptation rises up almost by the hour. You know I can't be everywhere. I can't keep you from it. But God—He knows your thoughts. He knows your heart." Pa held a finger near my face. "You're slipping away, boy. And God is your only lifeline."

I knew the hymn he was quoting. Same one we'd sung on Sunday. His revival meeting favorite from the Prohibition campaign.

*Throw out the lifeline! Throw out the lifeline!*
*Someone is drifting away;*
*Throw out the lifeline! Throw out the lifeline!*

Someone is sinking today.

That was me. Drifting. Sinking. I knew I'd done wrong. I needed someone to reach out. Needed someone to throw me a lifeline. Or maybe just to understand.

"I'm sorry, Pa."

He stared stone silent a moment, then said, "You're at an age, boy." Slowly he gave his head a shake. "Don't defy me."

# CHAPTER

# 9

Saturday morning I rose with the crow of a faraway rooster. I dressed quickly and crept with stocking feet down the stairs.

In the kitchen, I broke kindling. It was always my chore to start a new fire in the woodstove each morning, so I stacked some sweet cedar twigs over oak chips and lit them with a match.

Then I slapped together a green pepper sandwich on buttered bread. As I searched in the low light for a paper wrap, Pa appeared in the doorway. I stiffened. I'd hoped to have been gone by the time he awoke.

"Morning, son."

I was relieved to hear the slight note of reconcile in his voice. Even so, I answered with a wary tone in mine.

"Good morning, sir."

Pa ladled out a scoop of pan-browned coffee beans and dumped them in the grinder. The deep creases around his mouth and eyes gave him a tortured look, as if he was constantly burning himself on a hot coal.

"Going fishing, are you?" he asked.

I held my breath. He had every right to forbid me to go with Uncle Micah.

"Yes, sir."

He fell back into that burning silence. At a time when I naturally presumed I'd hear one of his sermons, he stoked the stove and set down the coffeepot and said nothing.

I folded my sandwich into a hunk of brown paper and folded it again.

"Shredded wheat?" he asked.

"Yes, sir. Thank you." I fully expected him to hand me the box.

Instead he put a biscuit in a bowl. He ladled warm water on it from the tin reservoir next to the stove's firebox. Then he walked to the sink and pressed the biscuit with the ladle to drain off the water.

He had never softened a shredded wheat biscuit for me before.

"Thank you," I said, avoiding his eyes. I dropped a lump of apple butter on it and began to eat.

Outside I could hear the crunch of river gravel as Uncle Micah's Duesenberg rolled up the drive.

I shifted nervously, wondering how I might misdirect attention away from that shiny Model A. My spoon clanked against the bowl. I slipped my feet into my shoes.

"Pa, I have a verse for today." Actually it was the one I'd gone to sleep with last night.

He nodded.

It was from Luke. The story of the prodigal son.

I took a quick bite, chewed, then swallowed hard.

" 'I will arise and go to my father, and will say unto him, Father, I have sinned against heaven, and before thee, and am no more worthy to be called thy son. Make me as one of thy hired servants.' "

Pa did not react. He stepped slowly to the table and sat. I only hoped Uncle Micah would not blast his horn. Sober, he wouldn't.

I looked up and gave a nervous glance towards the window, then back to Pa.

He looked straight out at that sleek Duzy. In the glow of a headlight, I caught the glimmer of a tear in my father's eye.

And I knew that, deep inside, something burned.

Finally, he spoke. "I don't mean to be overharsh, boy. I truly don't."

I never hugged my father, nor him me. Our people just didn't. But if ever there come a moment that we could've felt like it, I truly believe that would've been it.

I think he wanted to say something else, but stopped short. He could never bring himself to apologize, I knew that. But something hung there between us.

I could feel him watching me as I stuffed my lunch in the tackle box, grabbed a jug of Ma's lemonade, then pushed open the kitchen door. It seemed almost as if he wished he could be the one taking me out fishing.

That would, of course, have been the normal thing a father and son might do.

But not my pa. He feared water, not being a swimmer, I supposed. He was a dirt farmer by nature, not a man of the sea. He taught hunting and trapping. Bird calls. Tracking.

I did not hate him his harshness.

It was only his way.

Uncle Micah stood by the touring car with the side door wide open.

"Don't forget your pole," he called.

I spun back toward the side porch and grabbed my lacquered three-piece bamboo rod. A gift from Uncle Micah.

Even though the neighborhood dock where I tied my boat wasn't all that far, today I didn't mind the thrill of riding there in a shiny new car.

"Mornin', Uncle Micah."

He gave the back of my neck a rustle as I crawled aboard and stowed my gear in the backseat.

"Hey, Lefty," he said.

My heart pitched. I looked back at the house and saw Pa leaning over the stove. He could not have heard.

Uncle Micah eased the car back down the drive. At the road's edge he stopped and turned to me.

"I had a very interesting chat with your pal Skinny Lappman yesterday," he said. "I learned something I never expected to hear."

He pulled out onto the roadway, gunning the engine, letting the tires slip over the graded clay. At the crossroads leading to the boat landing he slowed down, but then he turned the car in the wrong direction.

"Where we going?" I asked, looking back at the river.

No answer. He fiddled with the pedals and shifting rod, and the car lurched forward, speeding on down the road.

# CHAPTER

# 10

I thought a moment, but couldn't figure his plan.

"Where we headed?" I asked again.

This time Uncle Micah turned and grinned. "New Gallia City, Luke. Slight change of plans."

I looked at him. "To go fishing?"

"We'll go fishing, don't worry. But not right off. Little something I want to show you first."

The iron-ore port of New Gallia City sat about forty-five miles up the riverside roadway. By the time we arrived, it was near ten o'clock.

The streets were packed with automobiles and people. It looked like maybe a carnival train had come to town, and the news'd brought out every one of the twenty thousand citizens and all their shirttail cousins from the outskirts, too.

I'd never seen so many folks in one place, all heading in one direction. Cars stopped, honking their horns, "Ah-uuu-gah!" while drivers shook their fists at groups of boys moving like stubborn mules, whistling and screaming, while others with their fathers in tow yelled and pushed to make their way along.

You might get commotion like this down in Louisville, but never on a Saturday. And never a swarm that bustled about as frantic as this.

"What's going on?" I asked. "All the stores are closed. Is it a holiday?"

"Big doings," said Uncle Micah. "You'll see."

He come to a street corner, then turned, heading right smack towards the thick of the mob. We inched our way through a sea of men and boys wearing dark suits and derbies or waistcoats and snap-brim caps.

"What is it?" I asked again. "A revival meeting?" It's all I could think of that might cause the edgy hoots and grinning faces all around us.

"Might say," said Uncle Micah. "It's religion for a lot of folks."

We crawled along the street behind a couple of other automobiles, while the men on the sidewalks passed us by. A policeman stepped over and yelled our way.

"Better off stopping alongside the hotel up ahead," said the officer, "and hiking in with the rest of them. Place is packed, and you don't want to be late."

"Late for what?" I asked. "Where's everybody going?"

"Going crazy," said Uncle Micah as the touring car jerked to a halt. "Hustle up, son. You heard the man."

We followed the crush for another six blocks, and by then I knew exactly where we were headed. I could not believe Uncle Micah had brought me here.

It was a lynching. They were getting set to hang a man.

He hushed my questions with a raised finger, only saying, "You'll see. You'll see."

What I'd see would be a real-life lynching. And, of course, that explained why there were nearly no women present.

I'd never heard so much cussing and swearing about some "damn yankee" as I heard uttered from that mob. I tried to imagine what that poor man must've done to cause all that hate.

Killed a baby, I soon pieced together. He murdered someone's baby.

"All I want in life is one thing," said an old man walking near me. "I wanna see him swing."

"Good gosh, amighty," said another. "He's a killer, I tell you. The Batterer. Never been anyone like him before."

My heart pounded harder than all those black boots on the dusty cobblestones as I culled up bits of what this horrible monster must've done.

Killed a baby named Ruth, I gathered. Pure and simple. Whacked it with a club the size of a tree. Fit of rage, I imagined.

I heard two other fellows talking as they brushed past.

"Boys rode the overnight train from Richmond. They only come in this morning."

"Yep, a last-minute deal. And they head out for Columbus right after it's over."

"Chance of a lifetime, I'll tell ya." With that the men hurried their pace even faster.

Imagine, I thought, coming all the way from Richmond, Virginia, to watch a fellow hang.

We shuffled along with the tide of people until we reached the scene of the spectacle. There stood a huge walled-off section of town, where groups of boys lined up trying to peek through knotholes in the tall fence boards.

"There you go, Luke," said Uncle Micah. "What do you think?"

"I don't know. You suppose they'll let kids in?"

"Sure," he said. "Long as they have a ticket."

"A ticket? They're selling tickets?"

"Got to! How else you expect them to make any money?"

Yonder stood a fancy ice-cream cart hitched to a horse draped in colored ribbons.

"Want one?" Uncle Micah asked.

Ice cream at a hanging? I thought. "No, thank you."

"Suit yourself." Then he pushed me forward, till I about tripped against a sign propped near the ticket window. And that's when I got the full picture.

Charity Baseball To-day, the sign read. Babe Ruth and the New York Yankees vs. The National League Champion Brooklyn Dodgers.

"Well, I'll be—" I said, and shook my head. It was all this fiddle-de-dee for a *baseball game.*

I looked at Uncle Micah who was grinning like a bear in a beehive. "What do you think, Troop?"

"Well, I'll be hanged," I said.

And I determined to never let on what I'd been thinking. Which I believe I could've gotten away with, except that I just had to go and add, "But tell me, Uncle Micah. Who's this baby named Ruth?"

# CHAPTER

# 11

Uncle Micah's jaw dropped open like a trapdoor.

"Trooper, I can't believe you just said that. You mean to tell me you come from the land of the Louisville Slugger and you never heard of Babe Ruth?"

"The Louisville what?"

He grabbed my neck and pushed me towards the gate. "Well, let me tell you something. Today we're going to see the greatest baseball player who's ever lived. Mr. George Herman Ruth. But most folks just call him 'Babe.'"

Once inside, the pure majesty of it all unfolded before me.

There lay a green field the size of six pastures. Down to this end it had a dirt diamond shape scratched into it and a couple flat-topped chicken coops where some of the players sat. Compared to the clumpy, cow-browsed ground where Skinny played, this was a king's garden.

There must've been ten thousand people in the stands and as many more milling around the edges of that green field.

Every once in a while they'd "ooh" and "ahh" over some little thing one of those ballplayers did.

I had not felt so much tingle-in-my-tummy excitement since way back when I saw the Reverend "Horseback Harry" Jubilay atop a prancing Tennessee Walker come striding down the sawdust aisle of a Holy River revival tent.

Soon enough, as the game got rolling, I learned what all the fuss was about.

"That there's Burleigh Grimes," said Uncle Micah, "pitching for the Dodgers. Spitball pitcher."

"Spitball pitcher? What's that?"

"Well, that's a fellow who can lather up that ball with a little tobacco juice or some such, and then make it dance and dip like a darting bush sparrow."

"How could anyone hit a ball like that?"

Uncle Micah pointed his cigar. "You're going to find out right quick."

In the next row in front of us and a few seats over, a small boy with a chocolate smudge on his face sat with his father watching every move.

Each time a different ballplayer come close, the boy'd call out, "Is that him, Papa? Is that Babe Ruth?"

And each time the father scolded him. "Set still," he'd say, "and quit your yakking, or I'll have Babe Ruth come up here and give you a whack."

I watched the boy hunker down and study his knees for a while. I secretly wished Babe Ruth would come up and give the old man a whack.

"Watch this hitter," said Uncle Micah, nudging my ribs. "Pesky little guy in the two-spot. He'll try to bunt."

I nodded, hoping I'd soon find out what Uncle Micah meant.

"Now, watch," he said. "If he squares around, see where the pitch goes."

The batter shifted himself sideways, and the pitch went right at his head. The man dove to the ground in a jangled mess.

"Ah, Grimes!" Uncle Micah roared. "You lily-livered coward! Throw the ball over the plate!"

"What happened? Why'd the pitcher do that?"

"Well, Troop, the toughest pitch to bunt is one that's up high in the strike zone, and—"

"Wait a minute. What do you mean, *bunt*?"

Uncle Micah stopped, then puffed out a blast of air. He ruffled my cap, grinning. "Troop? What say we just sit and watch? And I'll break the game to you easylike."

And he did. All morning long, Uncle Micah labored with the patience of Job, telling me much more than I'd care to remember. But I'd say I got the gist.

Swing the bat and miss three times and you're out. But if you hit the ball, run to the bases. And if your team runs to home plate more times than the other team does, then you win.

Of course, that morning, I did as much crowd watching as baseball watching, because it was all a pure fascination to me. Particularly that little dirty-faced kid waiting there like a chunky chipmunk to see Babe Ruth.

He didn't have to wait long. One more batter, then here he come.

This time the grouchy old man announced to the boy, "Yeah, yeah. There's your monkey-man. That's the big oaf himself."

I looked down and here come a tall bear of a man carrying a piece of lumber shaped about like a fence post.

"They also call him 'The Batterer' and 'The Sultan of Swat,' " said Uncle Micah. "We might just get a chance to find out why."

Before he stood in, Babe Ruth turned to the crowd, lifted his cap, and stood frozen, looking more like the Statue of Liberty. To a man—even the grouch with the little boy—they roared out something, roared loud as a full-blast freight train.

With a giant smile, he turned in a slow, full circle, then donned his hat. With his two bear claws he held the bat out like a fishing pole and waved it gently at the pitcher.

That set off another roar, echoing back and forth across the ballfield, building on itself like compound thunder.

Meanwhile, Mr. Ruth stepped up and into position to hit.

I may never've heard of him before, but I knew right then, I'd never forget him.

"Knock it over the wall, Babe!" come a cry.

"Knock it over Kentucky!" screamed the little boy.

Then I noticed something.

"Look," I said. "Look where he's standing. He's standing on the wrong side of home plate."

Uncle Micah just laughed. "No, Luke. He's on *our* side."

Babe Ruth stood ready to face the pitcher, swinging his bat from the left-hand side. "Do you mean—?"

Uncle Micah nodded. "Bats left, throws left."

And in later days, I suspicioned that that was the whole reason Uncle Micah had brought me there that morning. To learn this one thing about Babe Ruth.

Lord of Mercy, I thought, the greatest ballplayer in the whole wide world is left-handed.

And as Mr. Ruth glared out at the pitcher from the Devil's side, that whole wide world seemed to stop.

Mr. Grimes pranced around rubbing the ball between both hands, squeezing it, kneading it, standing back and taking his sweet time.

The Babe stood ready still, tapped home plate with his bat, then pointed the barrel of it at Mr. Grimes. And that started a whole new round of hooting.

Boy, I wished Annabeth was right here to see this show. I knew how she felt about baseball. And the way these two fellows peacocked about, it would've been as much fun to see her face as to watch them do it.

Finally, Mr. Grimes served up the ball, and Mr. Ruth swung at it. Swung so hard his whole body twisted like a pretzel.

But that pitch! From my angle—over near the first base—I could see it come hard for most of the way, then dip down like it dropped off the end of a table.

"Spitball," said Uncle Micah. And now I understood that.

Everyone shouted at once.

"Throw him a strike, you rag arm!"

"Give him a pitch he can hit."

Well, that pitch come next. Mr. Ruth's second swing was even stronger than the first. And the *crack!* It sounded like a hundred-foot oak tree had snapped in two. The ball shot up, and I truly believed it would never come down. To this day, I'm not sure it ever did.

Over the fence it flew, up a hillside, and clean over the roof of a two-story house. From where I sat, it could've gone on to circle the earth.

Babe Ruth started around the bases. He didn't really run. He moved more like a slow, tippy-toe dancing bear, letting everybody take a real good look.

After he'd stopped to plant his big shoe smack in the middle of home plate, the small boy up front sat down again, but backwards. He faced the hollering, backslapping crowd, all of us, with a smile big and bright as a shooting star.

And I knew then, that's what I wanted to do one day. To cause talk and sensation—and put a smile like that on a dirty-faced kid.

But at the same moment, I felt instant shame over my thinking. Felt just like what Pa had preached in his sermon.

As I listened to the hero worship around me, I began to imagine the very temptation Jesus must've felt when the Devil tantalized him with the promise of riches and power beyond belief. And I realized, too, the effect Annabeth's little talk'd had on me.

Right quick, I could see how tempting baseball could be, the frenzy it could stir and the Devil-like self-importance it could give a man who had a talent for the game.

On the ride back home, those thoughts rumbled in my brain like thunderclouds. I asked Uncle Micah to tell me more about Babe Ruth.

"He's a good man," Uncle Micah started. "Folks claim he's wild, going out nights drinking and cavorting and so on, but I tell you, he's got a heart of gold. For example, every penny he made today went to a good cause. This game was unscheduled until two days ago. That's when the New Gallia City Boys' and Girls' Home caught fire, and half the building burned down. Someone told the Babe. And he made sure the team train stopped here on their way from Richmond so they could play a special six-inning game this morning to raise money for the orphans."

"How much you figure they raised?"

"Shoot." He looked up, ciphering. "A good ten thousand dollars, I reckon. Course, that's nothing for the Babe."

I rode silent most of the way back. The left hand was the hand of the Devil, wasn't it? Sports was sinful, wasn't it? Then how could you explain a left-handed ballplayer practically rebuilding an orphanage in one day? I had a heap of thinking to do, and it wasn't going to be easy.

There I was, stuck smack between two worlds. Between my church and the baseball field. Between Uncle Micah and Pa. Between the power of my left hand and the clumsy efforts of my right.

And something else I'd seen that day had touched me, too. Deep. Deep as the Reverend "Horseback Harry's" plea to come up and save my soul back when I was eight years old.

It was the smile on that dirty-faced kid.

# CHAPTER

# 12

By the time we'd returned to Crown Falls, rowed the boat out and settled down to the task of fishing, it was about an hour before sundown.

Uncle Micah had waited all day for this moment, I figured, the way he eyed me quietly, then tilted back his floppy calico snap-brim cap.

"Now, Luke," he said. "I got something I need to ask you."

I tensed up a bit. "Yes, sir."

"Your pal, young Mr. Lappman, said something interesting to me yesterday. Said the boy with the best throwing arm he ever saw was some new kid from Kentucky."

I dug into the can of worms. "He said that?"

"Said this kid had a hell of an arm. Could fire the ball like a Chinese rocket." He lit a big cigar, took a puff, then tapped out the fire on the side of the boat. "Is that right?"

I untangled a lively candidate from a wormy knot in the bottom of the can. "I reckon."

"Then why in blue blazes aren't you out there playing ball after school? The Lappman boy said he tried to get you to." Uncle Micah chomped off a chunk of cigar and chewed on it.

"Reckon you already know why," I said, and passed the tin can to him. He reached in with his left hand.

"It's—you know how Pa is. He don't allow sports. Holds it a sinful waste of time."

"Sinful, is it?" Uncle Micah grinned. "Whole lot of adultery and murdering out there on the ball field, is there?"

"That ain't it. I don't know. Pa says it's like dancing or card playing. Just leads to other stuff. You said yourself, Babe Ruth's been known to carry on all hours of the night."

Now he laughed out loud, shaking dirt from his worm. "Baseball didn't cause that!" he said. "Why, you poor Holy River Baptists. You can hold to the stupidest bunch of claptrap I ever heard."

I winced at that. Not being raised to argue, I fought the urge to do so. But I had to defend my pa.

"It ain't claptrap," I muttered.

"It ain't?" Uncle Micah's face showed mock wonder, his eyebrows raised high like bird wings. "What is it, then?"

Slowly, I looked off down the gray green river. With all the gentle rains of recent and the snow melting in the uplands, the water ran brisk. And for a moment, I longed to run with it.

Uncle Micah knew my fix—how I couldn't possibly give him an answer he'd agree with—and he bent forward to bait his hook.

"You want me to talk to your pa for you?"

I glanced at the worm whipping and thrashing about.

"Wouldn't do no good. Pa, he's set in his ways."

"Well," said Uncle Micah, "so was this worm till I dug him up." He completed his task and shook the dirt from his hand. "It's a shame, son. A real shame what your pa's done to you."

I shrugged. "That's how it is, Uncle Micah. I—"

He shook his head to cut me off. "Oh, bullgrass! Listen, Trooper. Tell me true. Would you like to play baseball?"

I took a big breath. Somehow I just didn't feel safe letting him—or anybody—know what I'd been thinking.

"No, sir," I said. "I wouldn't. Was a time, I's thinking about going down that road. But, truly, I just can't see—"

My words fell off.

Fact was, with all my heart, I wanted to play. Specially after what all I'd seen today. But when I looked down the *whole* road, I saw more stones—and boulders—than I could overtop.

Uncle Micah stood fast. "Then I suppose you also hold to the fine and brilliant notion that left-handers are witches because they do everything backwards?"

I grinned. "Well, not exactly. Had a teacher in second

grade who taught that, though. 'You're born backwards,' she told me. 'That's why you're so awkward and slow to learn.' She even painted a red cross on my right hand to remind me which one to use."

What I didn't mention was how she'd whack a yardstick across my finger bones every time I forgot. Whacked them till they ballooned up and bled. I figured Uncle Micah needed no more ammunition.

"That was your pa's doing," he said, spitting brown juice into the river. "That was when they made him take that cinch off your arm."

I remembered that. The leather belt Pa cinched around me with my left arm stuck inside. Made my arm go numb, but it trained me right-handed.

"It wasn't so bad," I said.

That riled him. "Trooper, it was downright criminal!" He sneered his words, loud, as if talking to the forest behind me. "Don't it just burn your britches to remember all that?"

"Okay, okay," I said in a low voice. "I know what you're rooting at. You want me to get all fired up and spitting vinegar over what my pa and them teachers done to me. But, see, Uncle Micah, I put that all behind. Now, sure, I'd like to be free to play baseball. Nothing more in this world I'd like. But I ain't. Things ain't as free and easy as you might think." I snuck a look at the fat, busted knuckles on my left hand. "You're not the one who has to go home and live with the man."

He cocked his head, holding me with his eyes. "No, you're right, blast it. And I suppose that's what eats me up the most." He pointed his cigar at me. "But listen, Troop. You know, the Bible never does come out and say the left hand's the hand of the Devil."

"Well, it as good as does. 'The right hand of God' this, 'the right hand of God' that. And all those left-handed Benjaminites? Sure, they could sling a rock so perfect, it could split a hair. But they defended evil, despicable men. And that left-handed King Ehud—he was a sneaky, lowdown murderer. No, it's all through the Bible. The left hand is *evil*. And now that I think it through, I want no part of it. I come this far going right-handed, why should I switch back now?"

I put on like I *had* thought it through, but what I'd mostly thought about was all the attention I'd drawn just throwing that ball. And all the hero worship I'd seen at the baseball park today. And though I could *imagine* being a baseball hero, to out and out be one would take going against the very way I's raised.

Finally, I said, "Uncle Micah, I just want to be normal."

He laughed at that. "Normal? You call stumbling through life, hiding one full side of yourself, normal? If that's normal, then what the devil do you call me?"

He reared back with a great big laugh, waving his blackened greenheart rod.

"I call you Uncle Micah," I said, and grinned in spite of myself.

He shook his head. "Trooper, Trooper, Trooper."

The pole tip swayed under the weight of the sinker as he got ready to cast. Then he shot forward with a powerful whip, sending a graceful, swooping left-handed cast that ended with a *bloop*.

Then I, too, set to fishing.

I could feel his gaze on me. Sure, I thought. I can fish right-handed. I'll show him.

Then I proceeded to fumble with the line and hook, fumble with the rod and reel. Finally, I jerked out an ugly cast and lost half my worm doing it. I felt the heat of Uncle Micah's eyes, warming my neck, warming my face as I sat there, cross-boned, working the line like a ten-thumbed monkey.

And I wished I could disappear right down that river.

"Trooper, I never knew how much of a natural left-hander you were," he said, then looked away. "You're a *pure* lefty, aren't you? Just like me."

Yeah, well, that's the problem, I thought. Though I didn't dare say so.

"You know," he continued, "they tried that on me, too, long time ago. Used to swat my left hand whether I was using it or not. Said it was for all the times they didn't catch me. But, shoot, these days, most folks couldn't give a barn owl's hoot if you're left- or right-handed or both."

"My folks do."

He bellowed a shout. "That they do. Leastways, your pa. Hard to learn *what* that sister of mine thinks. But your pa—"

"He don't mean nothing by it. His way, is all."

"Yeah, well, his way has sure hurt a lot of good people."

With a sudden jolt, Uncle Micah shot up and tugged back on his fishing pole. "Dang it all," he whispered loudly, "I missed him. He was walking away with it."

I watched him settle back into position again, head cocked like a listening dog. Time to shut up and fish.

Everything grew silent save the lick of the river against the boat.

That was one thing I liked about fishing.

While you're waiting you can study on things. For example, the fellow sitting next to you.

I spied down on Uncle Micah's thick-threaded shoelaces tied in big loopy bows. And his socks. Not woolly gray like mine, but black and thin with shiny brown-and-white diamond patterns on the ankle bone.

And his hands. Wide-fingered, big-boned, ruler-whacked. Not the kind you'd expect to see delicately tapping on a typewriting machine.

Uncle Micah's hands had to *pound* a typewriter, those hammerhead fingers slamming out the words.

That's what I imagined as I watched him hold his black-stained pole in one hand and slowly slip the fishing line between his finger and thumb of the other.

Tugging a bit now and then. He'd tug at the line, then let it fall, dancing his worm along the river bottom, dancing it, I figured, as delicately as he'd waltz with some fancy, high-toned city lady at a newspaperman's ball in Cleveland.

He was a walrus, but he was gentle, too.

I saw all this in about two seconds, and then I looked away.

That's what I liked about fishing.

Next moment, I settled back and focused on my line.

Then I felt a fierce tug and *my* rod bent over.

I yanked hard.

# CHAPTER

# 13

I wound up my old Chamberlain casting reel with my right hand, trying to take in slack from the yank. The handle crank slipped from my grip.

"Turn that reel over and use your good hand, for God's sakes," Uncle Micah said. "You're gonna lose him."

"No, I can do it." Spinning the handle again, I skinned my knuckles against the German metal. My fingers fluttered like a scutterbug across water. Nothing was working right.

I whipped the rod straight up to pull in more line, but then I lost tension. The line rolled into itself on the reel.

"You're gonna snag your line," Uncle Micah said, sounding frustrated and fairly tickled at the same time.

My right hand cranked hard. I regripped the rod and accidentally nudged the thumb bar, releasing the gears. If only he wasn't watching me, I could've done it.

I wound again. And sure enough, all I could do was

wind that stinking, lousy line right into itself, jamming the reel.

I could feel the fish pulling, swimming back under the boat.

"Watch he don't get wrapped around the anchor rope."

"No, sir, I got him." Which was more wish than truth. Hooked, yes, but no way to reel him in. I snatched at the tangled bird's nest my spinning reel had become.

Uncle Micah roared and slapped his thigh. "You got him, all right. Boy, you got him good."

I near ripped the line in despair. The big fish started pulling the boat over the anchor line.

Uncle Micah bolted up again as *his* rod tipped. "Hey, now! Here we go." Firmly clenching the pole, he started reeling in with his left hand.

I was not about to lose my fish, tangled reel or not. I began pulling up the line by hand, laying it at my feet.

Uncle Micah confidently worked his catch, letting me fend for myself.

I was still pulling up wet line, hand over hand, when his fish hit the deck. A flapping cat, three or four pounds at least.

Mine seemed twice that size, as the line cut into my fingers. If only I could land it, I thought.

"Need a hand?"

"No, sir, I'm fine." It got harder and harder to keep lifting. Finally I could see it. A giant. Two feet long, swimming in a small circle.

"Careful, now."

I leaned over the boat rail to get a better angle. The little rowboat wobbled, listing low to one side.

"Don't swamp us," Uncle Micah said. "Let me get over here." He shifted position to balance the boat.

Just as I lifted the fish out of the water, it gave a kick and broke free of the hook.

"No!"

I knelt and watched it swim away, my hands wrapped in fishing line.

Uncle Micah only shook his head and whispered, "Damn."

I sat back holding the tangled mess. In my hands the hook swung slowly with a chunk of worm dangling down.

I blinked eyes brimmed with vinegar.

"You gotta tell him, Trooper. You gotta tell your pa so he knows how miserable he's making your life." He unhooked his fish, leaving a dark spot of blood on the floor of the boat.

"He ain't doing nothing to me." I spoke sharper than I'd wished, but Uncle Micah had no idea what he was asking. "I'm doing it all to myself."

I broke the line and threw the hook and sinker into the river. I could've thrown the pole, too, but I had the good sense not to. "I just have to learn to do things right."

Uncle Micah jammed a stick through the fish's gill and hung it overboard. He sat back and bit off another hunk of cigar.

"Trooper, your life's being run by a one-sided, misguided, straight-and-narrow-minded religion." He spat a fleck of tobacco from his tongue. "And you know what I call religion."

"No, sir."

"Religion ain't nothing but superstition dressed up in its Sunday best."

I grabbed the jug of lemonade. "Look, I ain't gonna argue with you."

"Well, you *should* argue, Troop. Blast it all!" Uncle Micah lifted his cap and wiped his arm across his brow. "And I'll tell you why." He replaced the cap over a narrowed eye.

"Son, I was raised just like you. But it didn't stop me from looking around, asking questions. For instance, your pa taught you hunting, right? Even showed you how to build a rabbit snare. But then, he forbids sports for some fool reason. Well, why don't you go ask him if he realizes God forbids his people to eat rabbit?"

"No, He doesn't."

"Says so right there in the Bible."

"Right where?"

"Leviticus. Chapter eleven. They're unclean. Not even supposed to *touch* a dead rabbit."

I opened the jug and took a long, cool swig.

"Sounds to me," Uncle Micah went on, "that like a bunch of those people, your pa's doing some convenient picking and choosing. And, son, that's the full reason why I quit the church. I's about your age, too. Those folks claimed they followed the Bible exactly. To the word! But I can open that book right now and read you fifty different laws none of those so-called 'true believers' follows anymore. For example, when's the last time they dragged a stubborn boy to the edge of town and stoned him to death?"

"Well, they don't do that—"

"Of course not! They pick and they choose. Well, call me a wild, run-amuck heathen, but I say if they think that book's the holy word of God, then they should follow *every single law* in it or shut up about it. You tell me."

I shifted on the rough wooden seat to escape his stare.

"Well, sure, it's God's word," I said. "Some of that old stuff, though—folks just don't hold to it no more."

"Oh, yeah? Then why does your pa pick this one old, cruel, *superstitious* belief about left-handers to hold onto?"

I pushed down to recap the jug, but the dang cork squirted to the deck.

"Trooper, look at me." He pointed with a blood-stained hand.

I glanced up as my foot felt around for the cork.

"When Moses killed that ram to make Aaron a priest, what'd he do?" Uncle Micah leaned closer and answered his own question. "He wiped the blood on Aaron's right ear, his right hand, his right foot." Uncle Micah did the same to my ear. Catfish blood.

"He was just following some old religious superstition against the left side. Same as you and your pa are doing now."

"But I could *be* right-handed." Good gosh amighty, I wished I never picked up that baseball. "If I worked and worked on it, I could do it. I'm just stubborn is all."

"Stubborn? Well, lucky thing you Holy River Baptists don't follow the Bible word for word, or you'd be dead."

I wiped my shoulder against my ear and spied the jug cork lying in the can of worms. But I left it set while Uncle Micah ranted on.

"Dadblast it, boy, it ain't a case of stubborn. Don't you see? You're *oriented* that way! You just plain are. Same as the flow of this here river. You can't up and change that. Listen, in the olden days, folks like your pa were afraid of rabbit meat. So they made a law against it. Afraid of left-handers, too, so they made a law against them. They turn against anything that's different and call it wrong."

"No, you're wrong!" The words come without thinking, and I regretted their harshness as soon as I said them.

Uncle Micah sat froze, gauging me, cradling his pole.

Even from a distance, I could feel his worked-up breathing hit my face. I had one chance, I figured, to explain myself.

I couldn't even look at his eyes. I scanned the vast Ohio.

"You think you're making good sense," I said, "but you don't see it how I do. This is my life, Uncle Micah. You think it'd be so easy for me to—to do what you want. But I have to do things in my own way. Because what you're asking means letting go of everything I've held in my heart since I's born."

He leaned over and spat tobacco juice. "Fine and dandy," he said. "That's just as *fine* as it can be." He propped his rod along the gunwale, sat back and crossed his arms.

Well, safe to say, that pretty much ruined the fishing for the evening. I didn't have the heart anymore, and Uncle Micah suddenly got a thirst that Ma's lemonade couldn't quench.

As we tied up dockside, I broke the silence.

"Uncle Micah, I'm sorry. I know you're just trying to help. I got some sorting out to do, is all."

"Forget it," he said as he wrapped a length of frayed anchor line around the iron cleat. Then he grinned. "I asked you to argue, didn't I? You made your point. Sometimes I just get flat frustrated."

"Sometimes I do, too," I said.

I knelt onto the narrow dock and set my tackle box and gear along the far edge, careful to place it where nobody might trip. Then I leaned into the water to wash my hands.

At this point in the river, where the valley squeezes up, the current ran swifter than most places. I tossed a chunk of leftover bread into the water and watched the strong current sluice it away.

A blue heron fluttered from a treetop and glided by. A big old carp raced up and swallowed the bread.

Then I felt Uncle Micah's arm rest down on my

shoulder, and he told me something I didn't quite understand.

"Everybody's got a river inside," he said. "Always something under the surface."

He stared out over my head, over the rippling current and towards the willows and giant cottonwoods rooted on the West Virginia shore.

I just nodded.

"Oh, and Troop," he said. "Noticed you could sure use a new anchor line."

I smiled, eyeing the rope. "Seen better days, hasn't it?"

"It has," said Uncle Micah, picking at the spliced and splayed line. Then he pulled me a bit closer. "But none as good as what we seen today."

When we got back home, Pa met us near the woodshed.

Oh, no, I thought. I'd clean forgot to bring in more wood that morning for the kitchen fire.

"How was it out there?" Pa asked, looking up over his reading specs. His kindly tone relieved me, showing no hint of the tongue-lashing I expected.

"Not so good, Pa." Slowly I held up the fish and felt instant shame that I was appearing to take credit for it.

He nodded, as Uncle Micah walked on into the house.

Then something strange happened.

As I knelt over a stump to clean the fish, trying to act as normal as I could, Pa come up to me. He put his hand on my shoulder. I could feel the press of his thin fingers as he squeezed. Gentle.

I cut off the head of the fish.

Pa only watched. Not a word. Just the light touch of his hand, gentle on my shoulder.

His left hand.

It scared me.

# CHAPTER
# 14

That day with Uncle Micah was another one of those turning days. Only this time, something had turned inside of Pa, too.

As soon as Uncle Micah left town, Pa started going out fishing with me. I never could've asked for or prophesied such a thing, but when it happened it come on ever so natural, that I never thought twice about it.

I reckoned he saw something between Uncle Micah and me. I reckoned he wanted to be a part of that.

First, all we did was bank fish, which keeps you busy casting out and reeling in, though it's not all that swift. But since Pa couldn't swim and had never been more than waist deep in the river—mostly for baptisms—it was a good start. Then after a while, we actually set out in the rowboat, braving the current and heading off shore.

Pa took a fair time getting his sea legs, and he tended to sit smack in the middle of the boat. I knew he feared it some, not being a swimmer and all, and I fought the battle of Cain, not to be so full of myself that I had to try and teach him every little thing. I showed him the bare bones, that was it. I let him scare up his own style.

"You say the good-sized catfish lie midriver, deep in the channel?" he asked one day.

"Yes, sir. Mostly they do."

"Then that's where we oughtta get."

I could tell by the way he treated the boat and gear, how he suggested we get a longer and better anchor line so we could float midriver, that he was catching on. That he could see what I saw in fishing. And it gave me a glimmer of hope that someday Pa might see what I saw in baseball.

The best thing I recollect about those days though, was the turning. The more time we spent together, the less harsh he seemed, and the better we got along.

Like last Saturday at the backwater cove.

In the spring, when the river rises, extra water runs back up the little side streams, filling the coves with backwater and giving the fish safe, calm waters to spawn in.

And when they come spawning, the fishing is extra good.

"That ain't right," Pa said, after I explained it to him. "They come here to create new life. We best let 'em be."

Since we'd just hauled our tackle a mile and a half to a good-sized cove, I asked him, "What if we only take one or two?"

"No," he said. "I believe we should go down and get 'em in the river where it's fair and square."

Actually, we ended up not fishing at all that day. Instead I spent a good hour listening to Pa sermonize on fair and square. But all the while I's showing him how to skip stones.

He even tried it himself. Like a big, bright Jack-in-the-pulpit flower, he stood up and showed me a whole new side of himself. And I truly enjoyed seeing that. Maybe it was the fact that there'd been a batch of new faces in church that second week, I don't know, but of late his spirits had sure been even-Stephen. And if there was ever a time to approach him on the subject of baseball, I figured this'd probably be it.

At one point, I almost asked, did he suppose he might ever change his mind about sports? Specially if I could show him how a baseball player might could actually do a town some good.

But then I resisted.

Fact was, I knew pure and simple how Pa felt about sports. A little fishing wasn't going to change that. And besides, last thing I wanted was to say something that might rare up the wildcat in him again.

So I kept hush and let things just set.

Which was good, because, truth be told, I was turning, too.

A couple evenings later, on my way to check my muskrat traps, I heard a huge commotion as I crested the rise above the ball field.

It'd been over a week since I'd seen that big game with Uncle Micah, so I decided to head down and find out what all the shouting was about.

The game must've had some sort of situation cooking. The fans hooted and hackled. Players, too, one team yelling at the other.

Hoping to blend in, I circled around behind the crowd.

I looked for Skinny Lappman.

Down towards the wood frame covered with chicken wire, I spotted him holding the bat. So I paused a breath. If Uncle Micah was right, if Skinny could really hit that ball as far as he said, I felt inclined to see it.

He strolled up to home plate like he was going off to chop some wood or something. Not a care in the world. He dug a little hole with his right shoe, then stepped back and looked towards third base.

Seemed like ol' Skinny knew how to peacock a bit himself.

"Up to you, Lappman," someone called. "You're the tiebreaker."

"Make it count, Skinny," yelled another.

He bent down, grabbed a fistful of dirt, and powdered up the handle of his bat. Then he dusted his hands against his pants.

Finally, he stood ready.

The pitcher looked in and spat. Shook his head and spat again. Then he gave a nod, wound up, and delivered the ball.

And Skinny whacked it. Whacked it higher than a red hawk flies. Land o' Goshen, it made a beautiful sight. It sailed and sailed.

Everybody sent up a hollering roar.

I saw Annabeth leap up, clapping hard. And that sent my thoughts where they shouldn't have gone.

Oh, to be Skinny Lappman, I thought. To be a ballplayer good as him.

'Round the bases he ran, smooth as a racehorse. All the way to home plate. Took it nice and easy, too, the ball had carried so far.

Annabeth clasped her hands and twisted side to side, sending him a big-boat smile while he swaggered to his team's bench. I could barely watch, fearing the envy I felt might rotten up my bones.

When things turned quiet, I decided to leave. But just as I did, Annabeth come rushing up and took my arm.

My heart thumped like a walleye flapping on the riverbank.

"Luke," she said. "You fixing to go?"

I motioned with my thumb. "I gotta get back."

"Well, hold your horses one minute while I tell you something." She leaned closer now and lowered her voice. "Did you hear the news about Skinny?"

I shook my head.

"Well, he's all fired up about this big-league scout who's here on account of that story your uncle wrote—"

"Good for him."

"—and there's a reporter from the *Appleton Eagle* that's going to come by to see him, too."

"Must be getting quite a reputation."

"And everything that goes with it, I should hope to tell ya." She smirked her mouth. "Skinny's at the point where he thinks he can hit a home run off any pitcher in the state."

I nodded. "He might could." How would I know?

"Well, *I* told him, maybe so, maybe not." She cast a glance towards me as gentle as Uncle Micah flinging his fishing line. "I said to Skinny, maybe he hasn't *met* his match just yet, on account of his match had just arrived." Her eyebrows rose like question marks.

She stood silent, staring at me, letting her line sink in.

I backed up. I knew exactly what she was trolling for. She wanted me to be that match. To pitch a baseball at Skinny.

I took a big breath. "You know I can't do that."

"I know you're not supposed to join a team and play sports and all. But how could one time hurt?"

"I'd have to ask my pa, but I know what he'll say."

"Then don't ask."

"I can't just—"

"Luke, didn't our talk the other day mean anything to you?"

I could not let her know how much. "What talk?"

She stepped towards me with a fierce stomp, bringing her face inches from mine. Then she glared until I had to fall back from the sheer force.

"Oh," I said, trying to muster my dignity, "about you and baseball and all that?"

"Yes," she hissed.

At that point, truth seemed my only refuge. "Actually, Annabeth, it meant a lot. I just don't know what—"

"Well, then," she said, calming her voice, "let me just tell you. I've never spoken so dearly to any boy in all my life. I figured a preacher's son might understand, might be *gracious* enough to . . . to . . ."

I looked for a rabbit hole to squirm into. "I'm sorry, Annabeth. You don't know how sorry I am. But I got people from all sides putting expectations on me these days. You, Skinny, Pa, my uncle, people from town—all wanting me to do what they want, and I'm in the middle just trying to do what's right. But the pure fact is, my folks could use a little extra money, so I'm heading on down to the river to check about four dozen muskrat traps to see if I might get me one measly fur to sell. Everything else comes up second to helping my ma and pa."

The crowd let out a roar, but I barely heard it.

Annabeth swayed back a notch and folded her arms. I knew I'd let her down, but dang it all, she wasn't kin to me. She was—she was temptation.

In an even voice, she said, "Tell me something, Luke. How much'll a muskrat fur bring these days?"

"Depends. Three, maybe four dollars."

"And how many furs do you take in a week?"

"One, if I'm lucky." What was she getting at?

"I suppose every little bit helps," she said. "It's honest money. Least you're not out selling moonshine like some are doing."

"Honest enough."

"What if I told you about a better way of making money?"

"Must be lots of better ways, Annabeth. But trapping's what I know."

"Maybe you know more'n you think."

"What's that supposed to mean?" I figured I'd said that a little too bold but, doggone it, I could sense a snare being set.

"Mean's this," she said. "There's a baseball pitcher up to Pomeroy who earns ten dollars a game."

I glared at her, but didn't say a word. She knew I couldn't do anything like that. But it sure sounded like a lot of money for pitching that little white ball. My mind shot ahead like a wild bullet.

There I was standing in my cast-off clothes with my paper-patched shoe soles, and knowing that every Sunday I'd see Ma wearing a make-do sackcloth dress to church. Seems we had a set need for every dollar that come our way and none to spare.

What if baseball could bring a little extra each month?

I'd turn every penny over to Ma. I wouldn't even touch it. And that way Pa could—no, no, what was I thinking? How could I do that? I couldn't even imagine it.

"I'm not saying any old pitcher could make that kind of money," she said. "But a fellow with a good arm . . ."

"A fellow could do a lot of things with a good arm, Annabeth. Including something worthwhile."

"You don't think baseball's worthwhile?" She stuck her hands on her hips. "Bringing joy and happiness to weary folks and such? After all, isn't that what Jesus did?"

I couldn't believe she'd said that. "No, Annabeth. Jesus never played *baseball.*"

"Well, I reckon he sure would've, if he had an arm like yours." Her eyebrows rose again. "You know how much money Babe Ruth makes?"

"Babe Ruth ain't a pitcher."

"Not now, but he sure used to be."

"You some sort of baseball expert, are you?"

"I know a thing or two. Babe Ruth was the best pitcher in the American League a couple years ago. Holds all sorts of records."

"So why doesn't he still pitch?"

"Well, pitchers only play once every few games, and he's such a great hitter they couldn't afford to have him sit out. So they put him out in center field and now he plays every day."

I thought a moment. "So Babe Ruth started out as a . . . a left-handed pitcher?"

She grinned and looked away. "And now he earns twenty *thousand* dollars a year."

I jerked my head to catch her eyes, to see if she was teasing.

"It's true," she said. "And with advertising and exhibitions, he makes over twice that."

Then she turned serious. "Luke, our season starts in less than two weeks. And the fact is, you could do a lot more good for your folks, and for this whole town, by playing baseball than by doing anything else."

"Annabeth—" I started.

"No! I've seen you run the trails, Luke. I've seen you chuck stones and mayapples. You're strong and graceful as a deer. You're a pure athlete."

"Pure *athlete?* Oh, come on, Annabeth. Aren't you stretching things?" She had the easiest way of making me feel uncomfortable of anyone I'd ever known. "Lookit, now, I gotta head out."

She touched my arm. The jolt lightninged right through me.

"I meant every word, Luke. I'm just doing my best to make you see."

I took a deep breath. "Well, you're doing a good job at it, believe me." Then I turned and started moving on up the trail. "But you gotta see things from my side, too."

"All I see is someone running away from who he really is."

"I ain't running away," I called back.

And that was the biggest lie I'd ever told.

# CHAPTER

# 15

At school the next day Annabeth kept off to herself, which suited me fine. It was recitation day, and we seventh graders were supposed to recite that Walt Whitman poem. I'd studied and studied on it, but had my doubts about getting it right.

Funny thing, because with Bible verses I could remember them all day. Sometimes longer. They're short and sweet. But a poem goes on and on and the words get repeated and it mixes you up.

"We memorize poetry," Miss Wilkens said in her high-toned way, "to gain the spirit and the perspective of the poet." Whatever that meant. "Poems are the chorus of our lives. The poet sets the words to the music of our souls. Each poem has its own rhythm that drums like a heartbeat."

She was rather strange on the subject. So, I saw, was Annabeth, who kept nodding at everything the teacher said.

"Poetry," Miss Wilkens concluded, "is full of visions pulled more from our hearts than from our minds. Our greatest poems are written in the dust of our deepest memories."

Sure, I liked poetry, but that about topped it for me.

"Willant Achsa," she said, motioning towards little Willie. "Please." With a flick of her hand she directed him to the front of the room.

Willie coughed into his fist as he slunk to a lonely spot before the dusty blackboard.

My guess was he didn't know a single line, the way he never took his eyes off his shoestrings. He tugged at his pant waist, looking like he was adjusting his drawers.

But then, sure enough, he lit right into it.

" 'O Captain! My Captain!' by Walt Whitman," Willie called out, fairly singing to the splintered floorboards. " 'O Captain! my Captain! our fearful trip is done, the ship has weather'd every rack, the prize we sought is won.' "

He continued in that fashion verse after verse, amazing us all, and sat down to a roomful of applause.

Hearing him gave me the confidence I needed. Hearing my name called next took it clean away.

"Yes, ma'am," I said.

I started off fine enough. Why not? I'd been memorizing since before I could read. But this poem—well, I skipped a line and tried starting over and—forget it, I was done for.

" 'My Captain does not answer, My father does not—' no, I mean—'he has no pulse nor will.' "

Miss Wilkens made a castor-oil face. " 'Rise up—' " she prompted.

"Oh, yeah. 'Rise up—for you the flag is flung—for you the bugle trills, For you the shores—' "

" '—bouquets . . .' "

" '. . . bouquets and ribbon'd wreaths—for you the shores a-crowding.' "

I stumbled along, stopping and stammering and backing up.

Maybe if Annabeth hadn't been there. Or Skinny, all grinning and sticking his finger up his nose just to rile me. I don't know. But somehow I jumped all around and ended with, " 'Here Captain! dear father! This arm beneath your head! It is some dream that on the deck, You've fallen cold and dead.' "

Right then I realized the only fellow cold and dead was me. I outslunk Willie back to my desk.

When school let out, I couldn't get down to the river fast enough.

No wonder I couldn't say that poem. I had so many thoughts to sort out, it was a wonder I could tie my shoes. Annabeth, for one. All of a sudden I couldn't think about her without my stomach sloshing like a butter churn.

And this baseball thing, for another. I never was the kind of kid—say, like Skinny—who could just flat out go off and do whatever he wanted, no matter what he was expected to do. But I'd never had so many cross-expectations, either.

And the more I let it well up inside me, the more I knew for sure. I wanted to play baseball. And not just for the reasons you might suspect. To me, it meant something else. I knew that if I could play baseball, I'd be free.

Free to be the boy I really was. Free to throw that ball as hard and as far as I could. And free of that old leather cinch that still bound me, in some fashion, even today.

I rambled over three or four streambeds, scanning my traps till finally I found one that'd been sprung. But no muskrat. At least not a whole one.

I pried the steel jaws open and a little leg and paw dropped out. A muskrat had reached in and got caught all right. But it'd only been trapped by its front paw. A muskrat will chew at its front leg to escape a steel trap.

This one had chewed right through the bone.

I held the tiny paw, turning it in my hand. From the shape I could tell it was the left paw.

I tossed it in the brush and hurried on.

Couldn't even think about it. When something like that happened, it was always better when I didn't think about it.

I went about checking all the other traps. Nothing. Then I hurried up the mountain to check my rabbit snares, hoping for better luck.

On the way, I spotted the cluster of mayapple bushes. I plucked an apple with my left hand, walked off, and fired it at the hole in the black walnut tree. Dead center.

The Devil's arm at work.

And I had to admit, in my heart, there was something else besides freedom driving my thinking. Money, the root of all evil. And pride. I was out to live a little higher, to hear the cheers from a score of dirty-faced kids. Surely to hear a cheer from Annabeth.

I threw with my right arm and missed the tree completely.

I spent a good while tossing and thinking. I nearly emptied that poor meadow of mayapples. But every toss was the same. I'd miss with the right. I'd hit with the left.

So was that a sign? I wondered. I held a mayapple and lifted my eyes to the treetops, asking the way the Bible did.

"Is this a sign that Thou talkest to me?" Then I pointed down to the valley. "Or was it that muskrat's paw?"

I waited, but my answer never come.

I trudged off to check my rabbit traps. First two were empty, unsprung. But the third one hung full.

A big rabbit hung snared, bending the tired little tree so much the rabbit's hind legs drug the ground.

Probably a doe, I figured, full of milk and babies. They really balloon up in spring.

Ma would be happy with this one. Lately she'd been getting wearisome of too much fish.

As I strode up, I saw something I'd never seen before. The rabbit hung by its neck in the noose all right, but its back leg thumped. She was still alive.

Truth be told, it was bad enough cutting and gutting a mother rabbit with all that dripping milk. Or opening up a pregnant doe. Those were other things I had to do fast, without thinking.

But when I saw this one dangling helpless—I don't know, maybe I was just too sentimental, maybe it was her eyes, big and brown and begging for help, maybe it was the fix I's in—whatever it was, I grabbed her by the nape of the neck, and brought her close.

"There, there, old girl," I said, stroking her furry backbone.

She scratched at me to get away—rabbits can scratch deep as a cat—but I huddled her in my armpit until she calmed down.

"How long've you been hanging there, huh, girl?" I talked like I was holding a baby. "You're a tough bunny, you know that?" I squeezed a bit, then I slipped off the noose.

"There, it's all right now."

It felt good just to hold her, to feel her quivering go down and a warm calm rise up.

And, like I said, on this particular day maybe I was feeling sad or whatnot. At any rate, I held that furry bundle and rocked her, and a feeling hit me. Right in the heart. Big tears come rolling off my nose tip, dripping down to her mottled brown coat.

And then I remembered something. Pa had told me they died instantly, that the snap of the snare broke their necks. Well, this was the longest instant I'd ever seen. And Pa had also told me rabbit meat was good meat. But I'd checked what Uncle Micah'd said, and the Bible held different. And all along Pa had told me that using my left arm was sinister, that it led to doing the Devil's work. But I'd seen with my own eyes how much good a left-handed man could do.

I saw clear as day. I was in the fix I was in all on account of what Pa believed. And Pa, I realized, could be wrong.

"Dang it all to *hell*," I said.

I crouched down and set the rabbit on the trail. She just stood there and looked at me.

"Go," I whispered. I tried to blink the bleary out of my eyes. "Just go." I clapped my hands and she darted off, zigzagging along the path. And I cried even more watching her run.

Free, I thought. Dang, it must feel good to be free.

Then I leapt up, jumped on the maple sapling, and snapped it. I worked the skinny trunk back and forth until it broke loose. Like a madman, I swung it over my head and into the dirt.

I struck it against a hickory tree. Whacked so hard my hands stung. I whacked it again and the sapling broke in half.

Right then it seemed like everything had turned crystal clear at once. My whole world had been kicked head-over-teakettle and come up aces.

Like that wild rabbit, I lit off down the trail, waving the stick, whacking bushes and trees.

When I reached the rise above the ball field, I marked the moment. That was the instant in my life when I knew I'd never set another trap again.

I could not stand the thought of me ever causing any living creature to be caught between two worlds.

That rabbit's eyes—the muskrat's leg—their images kept filling the picture in my brain. How many other animals had died slow deaths before I'd found them? How many hungry babies had squealed in their dens, waiting for their mama's milk that never come?

And how much longer would I hang undecided?

My blood was a-raging. I felt lied to, tricked, and used like a fool.

The first thing I thought of doing was running away. Far as I could go. To take my boat like Huck Finn and run down the Ohio, down the Mississippi, all the way to New Orleans.

To leave everything behind and start all over new.

And in a way, I did just that.

I come off that mountain and walked straight towards the baseball field. But this time I kept on a-walking. Like Moses through the Red Sea, I tromped clean through that game.

All the running stopped.

Shouting quit.

Ballplayers stepped to one side or the other.

Skinny come out and met me near his team's bench. He wore a big, hound dog's grin.

"Show me how you do this," I said, and I sent him the meanest dang look I could muster. "I want to pitch baseball."

# CHAPTER
# 16

Get him a glove," Skinny yelled. Some boy scampered off.

Skinny took ahold of my stick and tossed it. "You won't be needing this."

Then he guided me to the pitching spot. I heard Annabeth call out from the crowd, but I knew better than to look. A bunch of fellows rushed in around us.

"We want him on our team."

"No, he's playing for us."

"Hush up," said Skinny. For once I read the respect everyone had for him, including all the high-school boys.

"He'll pitch right now," he said. "Against us."

Skinny's eyes held a starry glint as he added, "I want to bat."

Then he turned and talked direct to me.

"Okay, Luke, now listen. It's easy as pie. You put

your left foot on this." He pointed to a battered strip of white wood sitting flush with the top of a smooth little pile of dirt.

"Then rock back with your right foot." He demonstrated as he talked. Awkward, I could tell, since he was right-handed, but I got the general idea.

"Then hitch off to one side some and pause a tick. Then you just come forwards and throw the ball—" He pointed. "—right to that ugly son of a gopher with the mask on."

Everybody laughed. The masked boy pounded his fist into a big round leather glove and squatted down.

"That's your target," Skinny said, pointing at the glove.

I felt like someone must've told him how good I was at hitting a target. I wasn't about to let that someone down.

Skinny handed me the ball and a glove. "We're between innings," he said, "so go ahead, practice a bunch. But mostly, you just step up, turn, and throw. Easy as pie."

I did, and he was right. Hardest part was having all those eyeballs on me. Best part was the hoots and stomps I heard first time I tossed the ball. What a sound it made snapping against that leather.

After the pitch, I felt a bit prideful, hearing the boys cuss and buzz among themselves, until the return throw hit my glove then skipped into my gut and fell to the dirt.

"Hey, go easy there," Skinny yelled. "He ain't never caught a ball before."

More hoots after that, and I humbled up.

I's definitely on display, but I tell you, I just buckled down all the more, focusing on that leather target and keeping the mean in my eyes.

I had to work fast, though. Mindless. If I'd stopped to think about what I's actually doing, I knew I couldn't of done it at all.

"You look goofy as a scarecrow in a gust," Skinny said in a quiet voice. "But, dang, you get it *done.*"

Then he added, "Our team's final cut is about a week off. And I do believe we got a uniform just your size."

I ignored that and kept on a-working.

After a dozen pitches or so, Skinny turned to all the players and hollered, "Okay, here we go. Our side's up. Top of the order."

Everybody had a place to run to but me. Suddenly I felt lonely as a lost lamb.

The boy with the mask come out to talk. "All you gotta do is throw that fastball wherever I put my mitt. You hit the mitt, and they won't hit you. You follow?"

"Yeah, sure." I didn't really, but I was too wound up, mean-eyed, and full of go to say anything else. I pounded my glove the way I saw him do.

I fought the powerful urge to look up in the seats for Annabeth. But I knew if I took even one look, I'd bumble and stumble out here just like trying to recite that poem. So I kicked my toe into the dirt and shook my shoulders like Burleigh Grimes.

106

The first fellow to come and hit was some little black-haired pip-squeak. I threw three straight pitches. All strikes. He didn't take a swing at a single one. Didn't seem fair, since he looked so anxious to do something, but that was the rules. He had to go back yonder and sit down.

The next boy did almost the same thing, although after the first couple pitches he did swat at the ball once. He sat down, too.

Then here come ol' Skinny himself stepping up. He stood a ways off, swinging two bats at once, and you'd a thought he was king cock in the henhouse the way the cackle and hollering rose up all around.

"Better swing three bats," one man called from the crowd, "if you expect to catch up to that fireball."

I didn't know if you could use more than one bat at a time or not, but when he stood ready to hit, he only held one. Nice turned length of oiled ash, it looked to me like.

Skinny swung at my first throw soon as he saw it. His whole body spun around like a long-shafted well auger drilling into the ground for water. But he come up dry.

A mighty swing, though. I supposed since he was entitled to three fair strikes, he wasn't about to get cheated.

Then, of a sudden, the Christian in me started to creep up. Skinny had always been good and friendly towards me, whether out of true admiration or from something Annabeth had said to him.

So I reckoned, why not serve the ball a little softer, where he'd be sure not to miss? Truth told, I'd a loved to have seen him launch one of his treetop fire rockets from where I stood.

Next toss, I eased off a bit. I was not disappointed. He whacked the ball, long and sideways, way off in the distance. It flew over the heads of his boys and over the crowd watching.

Not near the ball field at all, but what a wonderful sight.

"Foul ball!" a fellow shouted.

"Just a long strike," someone else called.

While two young'uns went chasing after the baseball, the masked boy come up to me again.

"Don't do that no more, you hear?" He put a scolding in his voice. "You don't need no change a pace with that fastball you're rifling in. You just keep a-coming with that. Hit my mitt. You follow?"

I nodded. His tone of voice made me put the mean back in my eyes, and I stomped around bashing my glove until someone fetched me the ball.

Okay, Mr. Lappman, I thought. This one's coming hard as I can make it. So just put it over the moon, will you?

Skinny grinned as if he'd read my mind. He spat into his hands, rubbed them up, and gripped the ashwood.

I rocked back, hefted sideways, fell frontwards, and flung the ball.

Skinny swung with all his might. I heard a loud

crack. But, heckfire! That little ball ended up smack in the middle of the masked boy's mitt. No rocket at all.

I'd struck him out.

Before I could go and give Skinny one more chance, the whole ball field was a-swamp with fellows running every which way and acrosst. And half of them come stumbling right at me.

Hooting, hopping, and hollering to beat the band.

"That ball of his come harder than 'Big Train' Johnson's!" one fellow yelled.

Someone grabbed me about the shoulders, someone knocked off my cap and tussed up my hair.

"We got us another Cy Young!"

"Cy Young, heck! This boy's a lefty. We got us another Babe Ruth!"

Over yonder I glimpsed Skinny slinging his pretty piece of turned ash as hard as he could against the chicken-wired frame.

Meantime, I got jangled around good and hard, back-slapped till I near choked. I didn't precisely know why. All's I did was what a baseball pitcher's supposed to do.

But for whatever reason it was, I had never felt so good, so accepted, so *normal* in my whole life.

And now that it was over, I could finally look around for the one person I had really hoped to see.

Back a ways from the green-board benches, Annabeth stood clutching her bonnet and peering down at this whole mess with the biggest cheek-to-cheek smile you ever saw.

Just like that little boy up in New Gallia City.

And I could see then, plain as a sign on a post, what I wanted to do with my life. I wanted to pitch again. And again. And again.

All I had to do now was square it with Pa.

God help me.

# CHAPTER

# 17

That evening the thunderheads rolled in. Big black mountains of clouds poured rain and shot out jagged lightning that lit the valley from side to side.

"Mrs. Achsa dropped off a rooster and three hens today," Ma said as she set the soup bowl on the supper table. "We had a nice visit." She caught my eye. "Luke, I found our chicken coop sorely in need of repair. All the wire's rusted up and come loose. I tied it down some, but only temporary."

"I'll fix it first thing in the morning, ma'am."

"Good. Mrs. Achsa recalled there being some extra chicken wire in our shed." Then she paused and looked at me—calling me with her eyes—in a way only I saw. "Need to put that chicken wire to its proper use," she said.

Proper use? I looked down. Did she mean instead of using it to stop baseballs? Did Willie Achsa's mother say something to her about the baseball game?

"No rabbits today, son?" Pa asked, ladling out the lentil bean soup.

"No, sir—I, uh—" I shook my head. "No rabbits."

Pa had a sense for detecting weasel-talking. I'd let too many of my thoughts show in my voice.

He raised an eyebrow. "You have something more to say, do you?"

As a matter of fact, I had a fair speech planned. But not about rabbits. And in my mind I could speak it perfectly. But at the first thought of actually telling Pa that I'd decided to be a left-handed baseball pitcher, my heart thundered and I stopped breathing.

"No, sir, I was just thinking—what Ma said—and how nice it'd be to raise a flock of chickens—have chicken dinner more regular. That's all."

He nodded agreement. "If that be God's will."

"Yes, sir."

Say what you will about Pa, but I believe all he really cared about was what was best for me. If I could only figure out a way to show him, I thought, that playing baseball could be best for all of us.

Next couple of days the showers hit heavy between short dry spells and even a bit of sun. Not enough water to bother you, but it did sog up the ground. And kept the afternoon ball games on hold.

Suited me. Truth was, I's anxious to play ball after school with the boys, but every time I thought about talking to Pa, my mind stormed with worries. And I knew I couldn't play another game till I come clean.

But that didn't stop me when Skinny scampered by one afternoon, between showers, to coax me down to the meadow by his house. To "work the kinks outta your pitching bones," as he put it.

Pa was off calling on neighbors, so I took the chance to let Skinny teach me something more about pitching.

"Now look," he said, flipping a baseball up and down in his hand, "a fastball's fine for a while. But sooner or later a real good hitter's gonna time it. And then—" He made a big explosion noise with his mouth and drew the ball up towards the sky.

"So what you're saying is," I suggested, "that the next time I pitch to you, you're gonna clobber it."

"What I'm saying is, you need another pitch. To mix things up. Like a curveball, for instance."

We walked beneath a buckeye tree where an old rubber automobile tire hung from a rope. Skinny twisted the tire so it set just so, then picked up a burlap sack half filled with old baseballs.

"Follow me," he said.

He counted off twenty paces, dug his heel into the wet dirt, and carved out a short line.

He pointed back at the tire. "That there'll be your new target. Now I'm gonna show you how to hold a curveball."

And he did just that, showing me how to line the threads along my fingers. We practiced some till I could get the spin right and nick that target the way Skinny said I should.

Each time I set that tire spinning, he'd hoot and holler an old song. "Saw a flea kick a tree, fooba-wooba, fooba-wooba!"

Which I guessed meant that the pitch was "per-zackly" where he wanted it.

He roamed around that buckeye rounding up loose balls, singing, dancing, talking like a snake-oil man to the clouds in the sky.

"I can see the future!" he said. "It's aces, Lukey. Hah! You're gonna mow 'em down for us. Team after team. All the way to the state championship!"

He bounced back my way to hand me some more balls. "I can see the fu-*chah*!"

"Well, then," I said with a laugh, "you must be a see-ing prophet."

"I am," he said. "I'm a-seeing a *big* profit if you keep on throwing like that. I guaran-dang-tee it."

"Okay, then, watch this," I said. I wet my fingers and tried something new on the spot. This time the ball curved and *dipped.* "How'd you like that?"

He didn't say a word. Just spun around on one foot, made a handclap and shouted out, "Whoa, *Buck!*"

I threw all afternoon, trying this grip and that, laugh-ing with Skinny and not noticing the time at all.

Catch me a bucket of walleyed pike and I wouldn't of felt this good. Here I was, making a new friend, making him happy, and proving myself worth something all at the same time.

As we finished up for the day, he said, "You gotta

come out here as much as you can the next few days, okay? Then I want you to meet our baseball coach."

"I didn't even know your team had a coach."

Skinny laughed. "Mostly don't. He's peculiar, I tell ya, but he's good. When he sobers up, he knows more about this game than anyone you ever met. But most times—well, this is just preseason, so me and Victor from the high school pretty much run things. But don't worry, when the season starts, Coach'll be on board."

Sounded like the kind of ballplayer Pa warned me against. I hate to say, but I fairly couldn't wait to meet him.

"And that bag of balls," said Skinny, "is always hanging in the tree, okay? We got a real important game coming up, in about a week and a half. Opening Day against the Appleton Red Legs."

Then the impact of what I'd gotten myself into hit me.

"We play here or there?" I asked.

"Their field. Coach has a flatbed truck we'll pile onto."

I took a slow breath. "Well, reckon I can, if I find the time."

Skinny held his stare on me. "You better find it."

His words hung like the echo of thunder.

I nodded.

What I really needed to find was a way to break the news to Pa.

And I began praying the moment Skinny left for

some way to do that. And I woke up the next morning praying the same thing. Little did I expect the answer I got.

Or that Uncle Micah would bring it.

# CHAPTER

# 18

That afternoon I was heading towards a little side stream to take out a string of muskrat traps I'd laid along the banks—my final act against trapping—when what'd I see rolling down the road but Uncle Micah's red Model A.

I cut across the field, hollering, "Hey, hey, you River Dawg!"

He screeched the car till it twisted sideways on the muddy road and stopped smack in the lane.

"Trooper! Come on, boy. Hop in."

I hustled up to his open door. "What're you doing here?"

"I'm working," he said. "I got a story to write."

"Thought you was all finished 'round this neck."

"Oh, a writer's always got one more fool idea to try."

I climbed in and he swung the car around, aiming back the way he'd come.

"Where we bound?" I asked.

"Appleton. I got a little surprise for you up there."

The town of Appleton was about ten miles upriver. If he had a surprise for me, I sure couldn't guess what it might be.

"I was clear down to Cincinnata," Uncle Micah said, "when the paper called. Casper said my ol' pal Chet Drinkwater, over in Appleton, was trying to reach me. Chet and I go way back. He's mostly retired, but, shoot, an old news hack never loses his eye for a good feature story. So I gave him a jingle."

"What's that have to do with a surprise for me?"

He turned with a hanging-jaw grin, like some smart aleck who couldn't wait to let the cat out of the bag, but had to wait anyhow. "You'll see."

For the next ten miles we talked weather and fishing and the great Babe Ruth. But Uncle Micah kept slowing down to look upriver whenever his line of sight would allow.

"What're you looking for?"

He grinned. "Oh, nothing. Just checking the river traffic. Old reporter's habit, I suppose."

Meanwhile, I was having a pure fit inside, but I never once let on. Then we swung around that last bend and spotted the Appleton dock.

I could not believe my eyes. Now I knew what he'd been looking for.

A riverboat! A big white-washed, side-wheeling, twin-stacked, double-decker showboat sat right there dockside, bigger'n a full moon rising.

"Well, I'll be whipped and dipped," was all I could manage to say.

Uncle Micah slid the car to a stop. "Didn't know if we were going to catch her or not. I must just live right." He gave a big wink. "You ever been on one, Troop?"

"No, sir. I thought they're all broke up and gone."

"Mostly are. But not ol' Sal here. Come on."

We walked down the ramp, and I could not peel my eyes away. The gold-leaf lettering gleamed at me. *"Sally Walk-the-Water,"* I read out loud.

"That name came from an old Mingo Indian," said Uncle Micah. "He claimed when that paddle wheel got to rolling, it looked like the riverboat was walking on water."

It'd been years since I'd seen a fancy-dancing show-boat, with its calliope organ music singing out, its bells a-clanging, and city folks of all sorts leaning against the rails, hat brims and parasols shading their delicate city skin.

But never had I seen one this close!

Uncle Micah slipped into the dockmaster's shanty and come back with a newspaper tucked under his arm.

"Let's head on board." He waved me on as he strode up the gangplank. "It don't leave for another half hour or so. Why don't we go have us a little look-see?"

Every inch was shiny and slick, from the pilot's house to the smokestacks to the twin brass searchlights mounted on the bow. Even the deckhands wore sleek white pants and billowed shirts.

Uncle Micah gave me the royal tour, pointing out the

dance floor and whiskey bar and moaning over Prohibition.

Finally he pointed his cigar at a spar-varnished bench seat on the port side. "Have a seat, Trooper. Ain't got much time."

I sat and he handed me a torn white slip. "Here's your ticket."

"My ticket? What do you mean?"

"Well, we timed her perfect. Drinkwater said if I hurried the Duzy along, it might work out." He nodded to the dockside shanty. "So just for fun I bought you a little ticket."

"You mean, I'm gonna ride on a—"

"Right. Listen, I should be halfway to Ashtabula by now. Ol' Sally here's going to save me the trouble of driving you back home. Courtesy of the *Ashtabula Star Beacon*."

"Uncle Micah, that's—that's *aces*. I can't believe it." I stood up and then sat right back down. "But will it stop at Crown Falls?"

"Sure, at the main dock, right in town."

I waggled my head. "But you said you were working. Were you just joshing me?"

"Nope. I'm getting to that." He opened up a copy of the *Appleton Eagle.* "Take a gander at yesterday's paper."

Right there at the bottom of the sports page I saw the headline. "Lappman No Match for Southpaw." Now I understood.

Chet Drinkwater had wrote a whole story about Skinny and me, the All-County hitting star against the mystery boy from Kentucky. I read a few lines, then I had to stand up just to breathe.

I whacked the paper. "How did he know about this?"

"He was there. Saw your little face-off."

"But it wasn't no thing. He makes it sound like big news."

"These parts, it is. Couple years and Dexter Lappman should be playing pro ball, heading for the major leagues. And you had him swinging like a drunken woodsman."

"I didn't mean to." I paced back and forth in front of the bench. "I was just—I's just showing off. I don't want none of this sort of thing."

He took the paper from me. "Listen what Skinny said. 'His pitch looked like a piece of white string coming at me. I never had a chance!'"

Uncle Micah roared so loud other folks turned to look.

Then he continued. "'Seemed like he was throwing off a mountaintop,' said Lappman, the finest young hitting prospect in the Buckeye State."

I felt sick. Ma used to tell me, "Be careful what you wish for. You just might get it."

Now I knew what she meant. At least it wasn't in our local paper.

I saw Uncle Micah tuck away his cigar and reach for his notepad. Then I put together two and two.

"You mean—you mean, *me? I'm* your story?"

"You're a natural, kid. So's the story. It's sports, it's human interest. It's David and Goliath. A great lefty who can't play baseball on account of some old-fashioned religion knocks out the hometown giant. I've got the piece mostly written. Just need a few quotes."

"No, Uncle Micah, no! Please. You can't write about this. I don't want—I never should've done it."

He was on the verge of scribbling something, then didn't. With a slow and deliberate motion, he slipped his pen and paper back into his inside pocket. Then he smiled.

"Trooper, I won't do anything you don't want me to. But listen up. I'm only one sportswriter in a country full of nosy people. You want me to sit on the story this time, I will. Mainly because of your pa and for the sake of my foolhearted sister who married him."

He stood, wandered to a brass spittoon, and spat.

"But I wish you'd let me," he said. "I tell ya, it's the kind of down-on-the-farm feature story the Associated Press loves to run. And if they do, it'll get picked up all across the country. Then people're going to want to come watch you. And some of those people could help you make a lot of money when the right time comes."

Money. Sure, that was it. Money was at the root of all this.

"Uncle Micah, this here's got me all worked up. First off, I ain't squared nothing with Pa yet. And second, if he finds out *you* knew before I told *him*—" I stood shaking, with pleading in my voice. "You can't write this story."

A loud whistle blew steam into the sky.

Without a word, he walked back towards me, his brow pinched, his eyes set on mine.

I believed he understood.

After a spell, he said, "They're fixing to shove off, Troop." He held up the *Eagle*. "You want to keep this?"

"No, you keep it."

He nodded, tucking it away, then buttoned his coat against the breeze. "Well, I'm heading home. But boy, I tell ya, I'm passing up a good story. Casper's gonna have my head."

"Sorry," I said. "But I appreciate it. I really do."

"I know you do, Troop." He hooked his hand around my neck and pulled me close. "And look, before I go, I want you to know something else. This river's a highway. Boats go both ways."

He pointed west. "I know what kind of life they want you to lead down in Crown Falls. But if you ever long for a place where folks'll just let you be yourself—" He pointed a thumb north. "—I got a big ol' house up towards Ashtabula way."

I didn't answer. Didn't want to even hint that it was a tempting offer. In another mood it would've been real tempting.

Uncle Micah snapped his fingers. "I almost forgot. There's something in the car for you."

He trotted off, and I met him at the gangplank when he come back lugging a thick coil of rope.

"What's that for?" I asked.

"I remembered the sorry state of your anchor line. This here's stronger and longer. Pure manila." He pulled out an end that'd been whipped with twine and dipped in tar. "Take a close look. Notice anything different?"

I held the honey-colored rope, smelling the strong aroma, like fresh-cut hay, rising from the fibers. Something *was* odd, but I couldn't figure what.

"It's S-laid," he said.

"Sir?"

"It's left-handed rope. S-laid, they call it. Very rare on the river except for anchor line. Got it down in Cincinnata. See how the strands run up to the left? Right-hand rope runs the other way. That's called Z-laid."

I hefted the coil onto my shoulder and studied the clockwise spin of the rope. Then, sure enough, when I looked at the mooring ropes along the dock and the hand rope along the gangplank and any rope I could see, they were all spun the opposite way.

"Uncle Micah, it's great. Thank you." I tugged on it for show, but I spoke without enthusiasm. "Just what we need."

"Great? Sakes, it's the best. And I expect to use it next time out. We'll float over the deep water and hook us up a few twenty-pound flatheads. What d'ya say?"

I couldn't say anything. My thoughts had already

spun way ahead. Here he was talking about going fishing, being free and easy, like everything'd be the same. But couldn't he see? Things would never be the same again.

The cat was out of the bag.

# CHAPTER

# 19

I should've followed Uncle Micah off the boat and taken his offer to go and live with him. I could've saved myself a pack of trouble.

Instead, that old side-wheeler pulled away with me on it.

The silver-piped calliope organ bounced into a catchy New Orleans rag song, a giddy jump tune I couldn't keep out of my bones.

An older boy and girl started dancing right there on the deckboards, and I had to look away. After all, looking had already gotten me into enough trouble. Didn't need to stir my mind up with anything else.

I was up pacing the gangway as the old showboat eased away from the dock, my mind adrift as I eyeballed the riverbanks north and south.

But what a sight. Steep hundred-foot cliffs, rocky shelves, and sheer drops with cottonwood, ash, and alder trees growing out sideways like so many fishing poles hung out over the water.

Later down, I saw slender farm girls herding goats and cows along the green flatlands, heading towards home. Their blue sunbonnets turned them into tall flowers among the high grass.

Every next moment, the scene changed. I just held the railing and felt the rhythm of the river carry me along.

Boys fishing, their straw hats hiding eyes that followed bobbing red bobbers. Faded, white-wood three-walled shanty houses stood hid in the willows where poor folks lived catch-as-catch-can, hunkered around split-barrel cookstoves. Vent pipes smoked, poking up like crooked black snakes from tar-paper roofs.

Every little once in a while I'd catch a whiff of simmering soup, with the scent of wild onions riding the sweet smell of turtle meat in the wind.

It was the great river. So much to see, so much to do. At every twist and every bend come a whole new scene to see.

Boy, how I wished this carefree ride would never end.

I dumped my new rope on the deck and pulled out a length.

Just for fun I lowered it into the water, letting the line play all the way out. The golden strands shined in the sunset. Seventy-five, eighty feet or more.

I pulled the rope back in, remembering to coil it backwards, the way it was laid.

As I set the wet bundle on the deck, I thought of a riddle to ask Chastity. What's always moving and always in the same place, too?

She'd never guess it.

A river. Perch yourself on a hillside, and there it sets. Reach out from shore and you can touch it. But get in and you'll see it's rolling right along. Never the same from one moment to the next. Rising, falling, moving along. High water, low water, whitewater, calm.

Uncle Micah told me everyone's got a river inside. Now I saw how that fit me.

I was always rising up one day, falling down the next. Moving along. Changing my mind. Never the same from one day to another, but, then again, always the same. Always me.

Then I realized what Uncle Micah had really meant. Of course!

The river inside us is our spirit. In his own way, he was saying, it's our holy spirit. A true and steady source of power. No matter what we come up against, that spirit will carry us along.

I watched the red-sky sunset over the river and prayed that my spirit would carry me through the rough course ahead.

Dockside in Crown Falls, the shore was a-swamp with people. I was tempted to wait the hour or so to watch ol' *Sally Walk-the-Water* take off again with her string of lights burning up the night, but I had work to do. I rambled down the ramp and onto the town dock with a little skip in my step.

"Well, now, I declare. I never took you for a riverboat gambler."

I turned towards the familiar voice and saw Annabeth there among the townfolk gathered to see the showboat arrive.

"How'd you get aboard that ship?" she asked.

I jumped to the shore. "My uncle arranged it."

"Your uncle? Is he writing an article about *you* now?"

"I hope not."

"Well, he should. My stars, after what you did."

"Did you read that newspaper story, too?"

"What story?"

"In the *Eagle*. Up to Appleton, they had a little piece about me and Skinny and what happened the other day."

She raised her hand to cover a laugh. "I hope they didn't embarrass our poor Dexter too much, after what he went through."

"I'm sorry about that, Annabeth. Truly."

"Sorry? Luke, what in the world for?"

"Well, for making Skinny look so bad and all."

"Bad? Shoot, he strikes out often enough, I hope to tell ya. Anyone who takes a big ol' barn door swing like he does deserves to look the fool ever' once in a while."

She grinned. Maybe it was the dusky light on her pale skin or something in her eyes, but for the quickest moment I was struck harder than ever on just how downright pretty she was.

"Well," I said, "he was sure a good sport about it. Even showed me a new pitch to try."

"So you're going to pitch? You'll play for our team?"

I glanced back at the boat and rubbed the back of my neck. "There's some details I got to work out first."

She reached out and touched my sleeve. "Does that mean, 'yes'?"

That set my heart to racing. At that moment I probably would've done anything for her.

"Annabeth, I want to, that's all I can say. But, look—" I hefted the coil of rope higher up my shoulder. "I got some work to finish up downriver, and it's getting dark."

The disappointment I read in her face made me wish I could stay. I quickly added, "But, tomorrow, um, I'll see you—I mean, at school and all. And by then I'll know—That is, I'll know more about it, and—and, uh, I'll see you tomorrow."

I made a step back.

She acted like I'd been talking perfectly normal. "Why don't you wait here a while and see all the lights get lit?"

I pulled in a big breath. "Truly, I wish I could." I was practically dancing from foot to foot as the idea of staying, then leaving, would change places in my mind. "But I need to go before it gets too dark."

"Too bad," she said, sending a long gaze towards the showboat. "There's something magic about lights dancing on the river. Something—" She looked back at me. "—romantic."

Boom. Seemed like someone had grabbed a two-by-four and whacked my head.

"I don't know," I said, backing farther away.

I hardly even heard my own voice. Hardly felt my feet walk. It was amazing how a girl could make you go from your regular self to a stumblebum stupe faster than a rabbit down a slope.

That evening, as I near floated around tripping muskrat traps and tossing them in the water, big raindrops began to fall. I hurried my pace, dancing more than walking. But every step I took that night seemed a jump-step to some ragtime calliope tune—and a step away from Pa and how I's raised.

And my mind set to paddle wheeling.

I figured tonight would be the night. Tonight I'd sit down with Pa and lay out the whole situation. After all, I thought, I'm thirteen years old. Near a man. Why should I have to worry about what my pa might say?

And why should I have to go all the way to Ashtabula just to be myself?

In the mood I was in, I figured I could do about anything. Funny how a little shift in thinking could make you see the world so different.

But on the other hand, I knew enough about the Devil to know that a shift in thinking could be just the way he had things planned.

And I knew enough about Pa to know—by the way he met me at the door, with the *Appleton Eagle* folded against his chest—that he had a plan, too.

My carefree ride downriver was done.

# CHAPTER

# 20

$P$a had waited downstairs as I walked silently up to my room and slid the rope under my bed. Maybe he wanted me to sit trembling as I heard him slowly trudge up the stairway.

I was too short on breath to tremble.

"Am I an unreasonable man?" he asked, starting off quiet and stern. Strange how his small frame could darken my whole room from the doorway.

"Am I asking you to do something you are not capable of doing?" The tremble was in *his* voice.

"No, sir."

"Don't mock me, boy."

"Sir?"

"I said, don't mock me. Of course you're not capable of doing what I ask. From the day you were born, you've been contrary. You came with a colic that kept your mother up all hours, months on end. Come time to learn the Word, you stumbled through every verse, showing no ability whatsoever to grasp the meaning or the spirit."

He circled me like a lynx closing in on its prey. Each time he made a point, he shook the newspaper at me.

"You ate with the wrong hand. You handshook with the wrong hand. You spelled your own name with the letters switched. You even tied your shoes with a backwards knot. If I hadn't taught you Bible verse after verse, you'd have gone twelve straight years without learning a holy thing."

I felt as low as the bug I saw scurry under my bed.

But that bug was luckier than me. He didn't see Pa bring out the leather belt from beneath the paper. The same belt he'd used to cinch my left arm. For years it'd hung on a hook in the hallway.

"The Devil tempts you, boy, and you roll over. 'Take me straight to Hell,' you might as well say. 'Let me squander my time among the heathen.' Anything the Devil wants, you give him." He flung the paper on top of the chest of drawers.

"I'm sorry, sir. I wanted to tell you."

"Silence!" He paced about, working the thick leather through his palm.

"I blame myself," he said, "as much as I do you. It grieves me to have to stand here and witness what you've become. But I let this fester far too long. I went easy on you. I pulled back from my instincts. I hoped you might purify your heart. But as usual, you did just the opposite."

He stepped closer and tapped the folded strap against his hand. "Turn around and hunch over."

I obliged.

The first whack across my britches nearly knocked me into the wall.

"Stay put." He hit me again.

Nothing in my life had seared and pained me the way that leather belt did.

"I had to learn the news from a parishioner," Pa said, using his harsh church voice. "A member of my own flock came to bear witness on what type of son I'd raised." He slapped the dresser top like he would a pulpit.

"On the Judgment Day the trumpets will sound and you will not be able to hide from their call. If you are gathered among the heathen crowds, as you were on that day—" Again he slapped the paper. "—mark my words, you will be left out of heaven. Left behind. Left outside the kingdom on Judgment Day." He hit me again.

I began to crumple.

"You stay put! Every act will be judged. Ye shall receive the reward of your unrighteousness, as will they that count it pleasure to riot in the daytime, *sporting* themselves with their own deceivings!"

He struck me harder. "You will have no place to hide. You will be banned from the kingdom of heaven, left to burn in the eternal fires of damnation."

He thrashed me six times in all. I expected seven. But I had not been strapped in years, so I reckoned that's why he'd come up one short of the biblical number.

I didn't know which was worse, the beating or letting him see the tears it brought. I just couldn't help them. All I wanted to do was shrink away, go hide, disappear. I could've killed myself.

All I ever wanted in my life was to be normal. To feel normal. It was my constant prayer. But on that day I saw I could never be. I would always go the opposite way. Backwards. And that would be normal for me.

I could hear Pa rustling behind me, breathing heavy.

"Set your left arm on the chest of drawers," he said.

Slowly, I obeyed. That's when I noticed he'd wrapped half of the belt around his fist, letting the heavy brass buckle dangle at his knee.

He stepped back, raised his arm, and come straight down with it.

The crack brought Ma into the room screaming.

"Ezekiel!" Her shriek scared me more than the blow to my arm. "No! Oh, dear God, no!" She rushed to me, pushing Pa out of the way.

The pain hit my arm quick, then disappeared.

She cradled herself over me. "No, no, no, no, no."

Over and over Ma cried soft words, catches and prayers, and calls to God. I gripped my forearm, hugging it into my gut, as Ma rocked me, kissing my hair, whispering.

Somewhere, in the hall or at my doorway, I could hear Chastity sobbing. I pictured her hunched and frozen, not knowing the right place to be.

My only thought then was, Ma, go comfort Chassy. I'll be fine now. I'll be fine.

It was over.

He'd clawed me. The cat had clawed me good.

Then I heard the belt fall to the floor. Pa slipped out of my room and down the stairs.

Ma held tighter, whispering, her breath warm against my neck.

Little Chassy ran up a-wailing.

I heard the back door slam.

# CHAPTER

# 21

I could not sleep at all that night. Whether it was from the driving rain or the constant pain, I tossed and rolled from side to side.

Ma brought me precious ice from the cellar and wrapped my arm in it. I couldn't tell how bad the bone was broke, but it was not displaced. My fingers could still move, though the pain was fierce. My forearm swoll up big as a fence post.

I had been wrong, I admitted it. I'd sinned against my family, my church, and everything I once held true and sacred.

Whether or not I was justified in what I did, still and all, I'd done it like a sneak.

And I felt worthless.

Even so, a low-down anger thrashed inside me. A righteous anger. An anger that would not let sit what Pa had done.

I kept asking myself one thing. If I was the most black-hearted, evil criminal you could ever imagine, lower than Jack the Ripper, lower than spit or dirt, would Jesus have done what Pa'd done to me?

If I could've even one time said, "Yes," if only once I could've imagined Jesus ever using force against another man, then I would've rested easier.

No such picture ever come to me.

By midmorning the rain had stopped. I laid in bed, not wanting to face anyone at school, and tried dozing as best I could. If I kept my arm propped, it softened the heartbeats pounding inside it. But nothing soothed the heartache that was bittering through me.

I wondered if I would pitch again. At least for now, Pa had stopped me from it. But he had not stopped me from thinking. And for comfort, my thoughts fell time after time on that afternoon when it was me who caused talk and sensation, who made a pretty girl smile and made a newsman take notice while I struck out the "finest young prospect in the Buckeye State."

By now, I had my plan. Head upriver first chance, by any means I could muster. I still had my last two muskrat furs curing, plus a number-one skunk pelt, almost pure black.

I'd take whatever the furrier would give and then drift about in my boat till I found a barge going north. I'd buy towage as far upriver as that barge could take me. And from there I'd hitch or hobo up to Uncle Micah's.

What would Pa say about it? Hang Pa. Let him twist

and turn on the noose end of a left-hand rope for all I cared.

No, these were not the thoughts of Jesus. They were vengeful, Old Testament thoughts. But I could not shake them. There even come a moment of comfort when I wished him dead.

Then I heard a tiny voice call. "Can I come in?"

Chastity stood near the open door with a food tray in her hands. "I brought some lunch."

"I ain't hungry, but you can leave it if you want."

She stepped carefully, her eyes aimed at the cider mug she'd filled too full. "I made you a green pepper sannich."

"Thanks, Chas. Just set it on the dresser."

I watched her tip the tray slightly to slide her chubby fingers from beneath it, then let it clang on the bureau top.

"Oops." She dipped her fingers in the pool of spilled cider and licked them off.

"That's okay, Chas. Thank you."

She didn't leave. "Luke?"

I crimped my mouth at her. "Are you gonna bother me?"

"No." Her bottom lip pushed up and out, the way it did when she was working up a good wail.

I couldn't bear it. I patted the quilt. "Come up here, Chassy Bird, and tell me what you want."

She took two steps and robin-hopped onto my bed. "I don't want nothing. I was just going to ask you a riddle."

"Well, okay. I didn't *know* it was important. Go ahead."

Her smile lit the room like a searchlight. "You have to answer this question 'Yes' or 'No.' Okay?"

"Yes. Is that the question?"

"No, no." She held up a tiny finger. "This question."

Her eyes moved up like she was looking at her chopped-off bangs. "Okay. Remember, say, 'Yes' or 'No.' Now, here it is." She smiled. "Will your answer to this question be, 'No'?"

I started to say, "No," then stopped, because that'd be wrong. But, then, "Yes" wouldn't work either, because that'd make the answer, "No."

"Hey," I said. "No fair. That's a trick question. Why, you little pip-squeak." I reached to tickle her.

She covered her mouth, scooted off my bed, and giggled all the way downstairs. I could hear her tell Ma the whole story.

I couldn't help grinning, but then I felt instantly sad. Once I hit the river, I knew I'd miss her so much. But just like her and her silly question, sometimes life comes up and tosses you a riddle that there's really no good answer to. Leaving was just the best I could do.

Later that afternoon, I stood at my window studying a Bible verse. "They have beaten me and I felt it not: when shall I awake?"

That, too, brought me comfort as I repeated it, watching the rabbits edge out of the woods.

I barely heard Pa step up behind me.

"Son?"

I closed the book, but didn't answer.

"May I have a word with you?"

I gave a little nod.

Pa took a long time to start talking. Finally, I looked up and saw why. His eyes were a-brimming.

He pulled in a loud breath. "I don't know what come over me. If I live to be a hundred, I don't reckon I'll ever know. All morning long I've searched Scriptures, searched my soul—"

I could not believe my ears. The room fell so quiet, all I could hear was the pounding in my arm.

"Son, I had no call. God knows, I had no call." He lowered his head and his voice.

Something squeezed my heart hard and tight.

"I was pure wrong," he said. "I got fearful, I suppose. Prideful, too. I got too overconcerned at what the new church members might say, how what you'd done would reflect on me. Then you being gone so late last night—I got all wound up about it." He stopped to swallow. "And I was wrong."

He took another deep breath that sounded like the sizzle of water poured on fire. "I'm here—"

But he could not go on. His cheeks ran streaming.

I couldn't bear seeing him break down in front of me. I felt like I had a chunk of apple stuck in my throat.

I just wished, for both our sakes, he would leave.

His head gave a slight tilt, his lips pressed tight and trembling. Then he turned and stepped to go.

But at my doorway he paused long enough to whisper, "I'm sorry, Luke. Terrible sorry."

# CHAPTER

# 22

After tossing sleepless for the second night in a row, I woke up Saturday morning with my final decision.

Sure, Pa's apology was welcome and Christian-like. But it was too little, too late. He'd restored some of my respect for him, but he had not restored a bit of my trust.

How long, I wondered, till his anger flared up again over one more little "backwards" thing I'd done? No, I'd always be contrary to him. I could not change. I would never be normal.

After breakfast, I pretended to go off hunting, but I headed into town. It'd be best, I figured, for me and the whole family if I moved along.

The furrier could sense my urgency, the way a dog senses fear. I had to take his criminal offer of eight dollars and fifty cents or walk to Appleton and try for better. No time for that. Besides, the money was plenty for a three-day trip.

I took the cash and my coil of rope and headed out to Hansen Dowdy's Hardware on Main. I decided to buy a good handline so I could catch fish on my journey.

And I figured it was high time to put the new rope to its intended use.

"What happened to you?" Mr. Dowdy asked, eyeballing my sling as I walked in.

I shrugged. "Broke it, I guess."

He seemed on the verge of repeating his question, then just shook his head and got down to business. "What'll you have?"

I set my rope on the counter. "You got a string handline fixed up for fishing?" I knew I'd be no good with a rod and reel, but even with my arm in Ma's blue cotton sling, I could drop a line over the boat rail easy enough. "I'll need a few weights and hooks, too."

He gathered the tackle and set it next to the rope.

"Fine length of manila you got there." Then he glanced at it again. "S-laid."

"Yes, sir. My uncle gave it to me."

He nodded. "Had to cost a pretty penny." He licked a pencil point and went to ciphering my bill. "So, tell me, how'd it happen?" Poor man couldn't help himself.

"A tree snare went off and whacked me," I told him, which was not so much a lie as a parable, I figured.

He looked skeptical, studying my face. "Tree snare?" I could see him trying to imagine it. "What was you doing, praying over it?"

I laughed as if he'd made a joke. "How much I owe you?"

He looked down again, ciphered some more, and circled the total. Then he spun the ledger and showed it to me. I settled up, slipped the handline into my sling and headed out.

Next stop would be the baker's, for a couple loaves of black-crust bread.

Soon as I stepped inside that warm, sweet-smelling shop, I wished I'd looked in first. Here come Annabeth and her mother heading for the door.

"Mornin', Luke," said Annabeth.

I quick turned my sling side away from her and dropped the rope.

"What happened to your arm?" she asked.

"Mornin', Annabeth." I removed my cap. "Ma'am."

"Mother, this is Luke Bledsoe. His father is the Holy River parson that took over at the old Methodist Church."

"Oh, yes."

"Pleasure, ma'am." I shoved my cap under my left arm, then reached out to shake her hand. But she just smiled and nodded.

I quick coughed into my fist. "I, uh, my arm's a little sore, is all. The other night, I's trying to, uh, do too much, and it—it kind of buckled on me."

Annabeth scrunched her nose and pulled back. "Buckled? So is that why you missed school? Is it gonna be all right?"

"Right as it'll ever be."

With a fumbling grab, I fetched my cap back out, then dropped it—slung it, more like—and watched it fly down towards Annabeth's feet. I bent to snatch it up, but she beat me to it.

Slowly, she handed it over, glinting a squint. With questions in her eyes.

"Well, I gotta go," I said. "Got a long ways—I mean, a long *list* of things—"

"Luke," said Annabeth, "you were gonna tell me something today." She paused, eyeing my arm. "Maybe now it doesn't matter as much. But, will you—will you still be able to pitch? I mean, before too long?"

I pulled my cap down over my eyes.

"Oh, sure. Why not? Shoot, this'll heal in no time." I touched my cap brim, nodding. "Ma'am. Annabeth." Then I hurried to the bread counter.

Not sure whether I would've told Annabeth much more if her mother hadn't been there, but I did feel bad leaving her looking so big-eyed and bewildered. With a quick glance up, I noticed her studying me through the sidewalk window. Almost like she was fixing to dart back inside and ask me one more thing.

Maybe in a few years I'd come on back and have a chance to explain it all. But at that moment, I figured, the less said, the better.

All the way to the boat dock I imagined my trip north, my new life, the letters I'd send to Ma and Chas. Full of adventure. Here I was setting out with nothing but a few dollars and the clothes on my back. And around the bend, nothing but pure adventure.

But when I crested the bank above the neighborhood pier, I got a sinking feeling. Among the cluster of fishing boats usually moored there, I noticed my rowboat was missing.

Oh, now, that's just grand, I thought. Somebody stole my boat.

Willie Achsa come rowing in with his brother, towing quite a stringer of fish. They must've been jumping out there.

"Hey, Willie," I called. "You seen my boat?"

"Seen your pa going by in it about a half hour ago. Drifting west."

"Pa? By himself?"

"Down past the bend."

I had a fair notion where he might be, but I wrestled with the idea of following him. And most times I would've just wandered back home feeling sorry for myself, but that was exactly what I'd vowed not to do—be my old self.

My verse for the day said to "put off the old man with his deeds; and put on the new man which is renewed in knowledge." I *had* learned a few things of recent. Things that'd caught. And I felt renewed.

So I set out along the shore trail, eyes peeled.

It didn't take long to spot him, coming back my way. There, about a quarter mile downriver, come Pa rowing slow and steady against the strong current. Truth told, he looked more like he was just thinking than heading someplace.

Among a thicket of willows I found a good rock and sat on it. I made a quick adjustment to my plan. I figured I could bide my time until he docked and started home. Then I'd grab the boat and head out. I bit off a chunk of bread.

Finally Pa reached the landing and tossed a rope over the iron cleat.

I watched a moment, waiting, as he stood and gripped the nearside gunwale. He held the boat's rim firm and steady, then lifted a leg and set it squarely on the dock.

Once dockside, he knelt down, reaching back into the boat, and fetched two poles—mine and his—plus my pine tackle box, and set them gently on the wooden pier.

Seeing how ginger he handled the gear sent a little twinge of sadness through me.

He could've been a great father. He had a good heart and a shrewd mind. He was a hard worker. But this man had a temper like a pine-treed panther getting poked with a hot stick.

That part of him I would not miss.

As I continued to peek through the willow branches, I couldn't help feeling like a sneak again. That's when I remembered my morning's verse. An old verse, really, but one I'd never quite seen the way I saw it then.

The Scriptures say you should always be honest, that people shouldn't tell lies to each other. And if you had been, then it was time to become "the new man" and quit lying.

Hiding there in those willow shoots, getting set to run off, I saw that I's fixing to do what I'd always done. Run away and hide from who I really was.

And I saw exactly what my life had been.

A lie. Always pretending to be something I wasn't.

And dang it all, I thought. Was I going to keep on lying? Just slip away like some Judas and never face my father again?

Or was I going to "put off the old man and put on the new man" like the Bible told?

The answer come free and easy.

I stood—*renewed in knowledge*—and walked straight down that riverbank towards Pa, forcing my breath in and out and ignoring the booming in my chest.

# CHAPTER

# 2 3

As I hit the wooden planks, Pa looked up from the end of the dock. By the time I stood before him, face-to-face, I knew I was not my old self. That part of me had been left in the willow banks.

"Son." He greeted me friendly enough.

"Hey, Pa."

He sent my new rope a quick glance. "I didn't expect you'd want to go out fishing," he said, "or I would've waited till you came home." He turned and set my pole and tackle box behind him. "You can fish here off the end of the pier, I suppose."

"Well, sir, I don't care to go fishing right now."

"No?" Then he caught sight of the bread in my sling. "What then?"

I looked upriver before I spoke.

"Pa, I had planned to run off. I planned to head up north and make my own way from now on."

His head gave a little jerk forward to study me.

"Now, you know," he said, "where that kind of thinking comes from."

"Well, sir, maybe I do and maybe I don't. But I'll tell you what I do know. I was wrong to think it. I was wrong to want to slip away like that just on account of what you done to me."

I judged by the squint in his eyes that he was giving my words a rigorous listening-to.

So I went on. "And I'm standing here now to tell you something I've been tossing and turning with for weeks."

That stirred him a bit. "I'll ask you to watch your tone, son."

"Yes, sir," I said. "I will."

He nodded.

Then I lifted my left arm. And I whispered.

"This arm is going to mend. And when it does, I aim to write with it, I aim to fish with it, and I aim to pitch baseball with it."

I don't believe I could've shocked him more if I'd taken out a gun and shot him.

"You aim to do *what*?"

I pressed ahead. "And if you want to boot me out of the house, then go head on. I'll live in these woods, I'll live off the river, I'll go live with Uncle Micah. But wherever I go, Pa, I'm going to be myself."

Now he was breathing harder than me.

I didn't know where all those words'd come from—they weren't the ones I'd planned at all. Even so, I poured out every bit of feeling that'd been cooking up inside me for the past week.

Now we both knew where I stood, which was all I'd ever wanted to do. The future was up to him.

His hand gripped his jaw and squeezed. "You finished?" he asked.

"Yes, sir."

I could see his nose flare wide as he gathered wind to speak. "Then you listen up. No son of mine will shame his family by living the Devil's way. You hear? If you take this step, I'll not force you to leave. No, sir. I won't make it that easy on you." Then he leveled his eyes at me like double gun barrels. "But as far as I'm concerned, I will no longer have a son."

"Pa, you don't understand what all I've been through."

"I understand better'n you know. I understand you're giving into a carnal weakness. A pure animal weakness."

"Pa, I's *born* this way. I'm a left-handed boy!"

He grabbed me by the shirt collar. "You were *not* born that way. You *chose* to defy me."

"You're crazy!" I said, backing up. "You're flat bone-crazy." I tried to pull free, but he yanked me close.

He lifted his hand, his fist tight. "You hold still and you listen to me, or—"

"Or you'll what?" I stood tall. "Break my other arm? Go ahead. Hit a crippled boy. Is that what you figure Jesus would do?"

For an eternal moment, no one moved. The both of us stood there, looking hard, eye to eye.

Finally, Pa lowered his hand.

"Luke," he said, "this is all—You're acting plain *foolish*. This here's—this is your Uncle Micah talking. It doesn't come from you." He set me loose.

"Yes, it does, Pa. It come straight out of me. I'm just sorry it took me so long to say it."

Then I spied his stringer of fish. Each one fair-sized or better.

"Pa, you spent a whole afternoon one time talking to me about being fair and square. To give everything in nature a fighting chance." I saw a glint of remembering in his eyes. "Well, that's all I'm asking here. This is *my* nature. I can't live your way anymore. It just ain't fair."

With that, I turned and walked away, leaving him to stare into the gun-blast echo of my words.

I didn't presume I'd said enough to convince him, but I purely hoped I'd made him stop and think.

And I had to admit it. I—this new me—I was feeling sort of proud of myself. Proud of what I'd gone and done.

Felt proud for about five seconds, too, till I heard my tackle box get kicked. Then I spun back around, feeling gutsy enough to curse if I had to. But danged if I didn't see Pa stumbling over that fool box.

Then he fell headfirst off the end of the pier.

# CHAPTER

# 24

**P**a!" I yelled. I ran back down the boat dock.

By the time I reached the end of the landing, he was flailing in the water about ten feet away, fighting the best he could. The tackle box floated alongside him.

"Grab that box, Pa," I shouted. "I got a rope!"

He sent me a wild-eyed look. I considered jumping in, but I was no great swimmer, and with only one arm, I couldn't swim any better than he could.

I knelt down and pulled out a length of my rope. Glancing up, I saw Pa bob underwater, pulling the tackle box with him, then break the surface again.

He looked at me with those wild, panicking eyes once more. Eyes you'd never want to see on a man.

"Kick, Pa, and hold that box," I shouted. "Fill up your lungs and kick with your feet. Here's a rope!"

He kicked away and whacked the water with his free arm. Trouble was, with the channel current and all, he was starting to drift downriver.

I wrapped one end of the rope around me and set the rest of the coil in my right hand, turned so it would play out easy when I threw it.

"Pa! Look over here. Catch the rope."

I said a prayer, then slung the bundle towards him as hard as I could. It flew about halfway, then snagged and fell to the water.

"Hold on!" I yanked it back in and ripped at the snag with my one good hand to pull it free. But every second Pa was drifting farther out and farther down the river.

I needed something heavier.

I ran back to shore and found a good-sized river cobble. If I could tie the stone to the rope as a deadweight, I could toss the line far enough to reach him.

But I was spitting cusswords trying to tie that rope with only one hand. I peeled the sling off and threw it down.

"Help, Luke!" Pa's voice come tired and full of wind. Now he'd drifted so far from the end of the pier that I was better off trying to reach him from down shore.

Finally, I rolled the rock into the rope and wound it up several times. I tried to knot it using both hands. The pain was fierce—like fishhooks ripping at my flesh in all directions—but I had to do it. I was using my arm like it wasn't broke at all.

Then an idea hit me. The sling!

That was it. I had to try it.

I shook the rock free and set it inside the blue sling.

Sucking breath with the pain of each tiny motion, I looped the rope around the sling knot and tied it off. I tied through the torture of it, crying and screaming, screaming at my fingers to get them to work.

Finally, I'd rigged up something like what David might've flung at Goliath.

I jumped up and rabbitted down the trail, trying to outrun the current. Every step jarred my arm and sent pain all through me. I ran harder, tucking my arm against my side.

"Pa, get ready!" I hollered. "Catch the line when it comes."

I ran into the river as far as I dared and set my feet in the mud. I knew I'd have to throw over his head and let the line fall on him. I'd thrown hundreds of stones with my right arm. I figured I could do this.

I twirled the sling over my head, hearing it flap as it whipped around. In my mind I marked the point of release.

And with all my might I flung it.

The rope flew through the air. The sling sailed like a great blue heron, flapping hard into the wind.

The wind. As soon as I heard that loud flutter, I knew my throw would come up short. It did—by just a few feet.

Pa dipped underwater, then splashed to the surface again. Was he giving up?

"Hold on, Pa," I cried. "Kick!"

I gathered the line back in, and with it come the only choice I had left.

I had to throw with my natural hand.

Back on shore, I found another stone. I quick unstrung the sling and tied the stone to the rope. By then my arm felt dead to the knifing pain. Or was it my brain that'd gone numb?

Pa was bobbing and splashing with both arms now. No box in sight.

I loosened the slack in my line so there'd be no snag. I'd once tossed a baseball more than three times as far as I needed to throw here. Broke arm or not, I knew I had to do it again.

With my left hand, I gripped the rock. This time I planted my feet on the edge of a small bank as Pa drifted into range.

"Pa, look up! Here comes!"

I hitched sideways and heaved with all my might.

A piercing pain shot through me. It come with the snap I heard.

I screamed at the top of my lungs. Eyes closed and screaming, I grabbed my left forearm and instantly felt the jagged bone sticking out through my skin.

I heard the stone splash about ten feet away. It had gone straight up.

And nowhere.

The force of the throw had shattered my bone.

"Pa," I shouted. "Pa!" I squinted through the dead, numb rack of agony. "Nooo! God, no!"

He was gone.

I splashed into the river and fell underwater. The current washed against me as I staggered to my feet. "Pa!"

I blinked over and over, scanning the water, but couldn't see what I needed to see.

The river—my river, the great Ohio—flowed calm and gentle, flowed like the warm blood pouring down my arm. It flowed and showed no sign at all of what it'd just done.

I couldn't speak, couldn't cry, couldn't think.

Farther into the river I ran, staring, stumbling, going black from pain.

From somewheres I heard a ghostly call. Footsteps. Someone shrieked my name.

"Pa!" I could barely spit out the word.

I tripped, then caught myself, only to fall again. I breathed in water and coughed.

Darkness come. Dizziness. Everything was fading away.

I had no balance, no will, no battle left in me at all.

Mud swallowed my feet and I fell a third time into the black of the river.

Hands. Someone's hands. Pulling me back.

Darkness.

# CHAPTER

# 25

**W**hen I finally woke, it was early morning. My left arm was wrapped up good and thick. I had a foggy notion the doctor had been there, tending me, and had given me something so I could sleep, but I didn't remember much else.

"Ma, he's awake," Chastity called.

She leapt up from a bedside stool and ran down the hall. "Just like I was praying, Mama. He opened his eyes."

My neck throbbed as I sat up and looked around. The sharp light of sunrise leaked around the window blind. After a few groggy moments, I tried to get up out of bed, but had to lay back down. Somewhere a rooster crowed.

Ma appeared at my door, paused, then hurried in.

One glance and I could tell she'd been seeing the world through teary red eyes for a while now. I'd been to enough funerals to know the eyes of a new widow.

Then it all come back. Pa. The river. The darkness.

And I knew he was gone. That it had not been some dream.

"Good morning, Luke. How're you feeling?" Ma lifted my covers, then retucked them.

I could barely look at her. "Fair enough, ma'am."

Chastity stood quiet behind her, watching.

"You slept a good long while." She pressed her palm against my forehead. "Must be good and hungry by now."

Food didn't seem to be much on my mind.

"Some," I said. "How long—" I rubbed my face slow and hard. "How long's it been?"

"You've been lying here over two days now."

She sat alongside and draped her arm around me, one hand to my face. Just the cool touch of her fingertips brought up the tears in me. I turned, hoping to keep them to myself. For quite a spell, none of us spoke.

Finally, I couldn't hold back. "Ma, I done everything I could."

She breathed deep. "You did, son. You did your best."

"I tried. I really tried."

"We know, Luke. We know all about it."

I believed she did, but I had no idea how.

"I never meant to cause him so much trouble, Ma." The apple in my throat come back hard. "But I'm . . . I'm like you said. I got a rebel streak in me. I'm worthless."

"Now, you hush with that talk," she said softly. "God has never made a worthless thing, and that certainly includes you. It's prideful to think otherwise. What happened was something we can't explain. The Lord works in His own mysterious way."

I reckoned she was right. In a world where you could be yanked off a trail and get your neck snapped or yanked out of the water with a hook in your mouth or yanked from one house to the next, one town to the next, one world to the next, at any time—seemed to me any sense behind it all was a pure mystery.

Then Ma gently combed back my hair with her hands.

"Luke," she said, "if you can take a visitor, there's someone here who'd surely like to see you."

"Right now? Who?"

Ma's voice actually had a little sing to it. "She's stayed over now for a couple of nights. I made her down a pallet in the parlor. Can't say what a blessing she's been, baking and tending and such. Your friend Annabeth Quinn, from school."

Ma read the puzzle on my face. "She saved you at the river, Luke. She saw what happened from somewhere up on the hillside and came running down to help."

"She did?" So it was her hands. Her hands had grabbed me.

"Chastity, darling, will you run fetch Annabeth?"

In a flash, little Chassy dashed out the door.

Then Ma's tone turned matter of fact, almost like she was reading the morning paper.

"Deacon Booker drove up from Memphis to pay his

respects. And to politely inform us that we'd no longer be able to live here in the parsonage, now that the parson is dead."

I guessed he'd have to say that. They'd have to make way for a new preacher.

"What're we supposed to do, then?" I asked.

"We have a few weeks to prepare. But after that—well, Micah has generously offered to take us in."

I could tell by the way the calm come back to her face that this plan suited Ma just fine. "We'll head north once all the arrangements can be made."

Presently we heard footsteps in the hall.

Annabeth come shyly at first, puffy-eyed from sleep, her dress rumpled. She stood barefoot at the foot of my bed. And I could not imagine a more welcome—or beautiful—sight.

Without a word, Ma took Chastity's hand and left us alone.

Annabeth leaned over the maple bed frame. "I'm so sorry about your father, Luke."

I sat blank a moment, then wondered again if there might've been anything else I could've done to save him.

"But you were a hero," she said, "a regular hero, for what you did."

I turned my head. "Not hardly. Heroes save people."

"Sometimes they do. But mostly, heroes just try and help."

I watched as her fingertips slid up the carved bedpost and rested on the rounded top.

"Sounds like what you did for me," I said.

Annabeth shrugged a shoulder. "At the bakery, when everything you said came out so weasel-worded, I got me a hunch that you might be up to something. And so I followed you."

"Then you heard what I told Pa?"

She shook her head. "Not really. I was up too high on the cliff. But I think I got the sense of it."

We studied each other a moment, and I realized there was nothing more I could say.

"Luke, you can't blame yourself for what happened. I saw him trip and fall. And as I came climbing down, I saw you doing every single thing you could."

I set still, saying nothing, trying to breathe away the shudders rising up inside.

With a small turn of her hand, she pointed towards my bundled arm. "And look here, Luke Bledsoe. Soon as that heals, I expect you to be back—"

"Annabeth," I blurted out. "Please, no. Please, let it be. This arm's given me nothing but trouble my whole life."

She took a long breath, and I could hear the weariness in her. "I know," she said. "But can't you see, Luke? All that trouble was none of your doing."

"Well, maybe, maybe not. But I sure added to it."

"So? So, now what? Are you gonna give up?" Her question come more like a challenge.

I took a long look at my arm. "What'd the doctor say?"

"Oh, what's an old sawbones doctor know? Luke, you tell me what your heart says."

I could not look at her and answer. I turned to the window, turning over in my mind everything that'd happened.

"My heart—" I said. "This moment, I don't know how much heart I got left."

She softened her voice. "But I saw you take your stand, Luke. You had the heart to do that."

I met her eyes. "But that was *before.*"

She stepped closer. "Yes. And now you want to go backwards. Don't you see, Luke? Here's your chance to move ahead. To press *on.*"

I lowered into my pillow. She was only reminding me of something I already knew full well.

And I knew, as well, the words she wanted to hear. They were the same ones I wanted to say.

"In my heart, Annabeth, I believe I'd like to take and pitch that baseball a few more times before I die."

She smiled. That same big, crackerjack smile that I'd seen the day I pitched against Skinny.

"Then I'll tell you what the doctor said, Luke. He told me, when a bone mends it comes back stronger than it ever was. Said, by this time next year you should be striking out any boy named 'Dexter' in the state!"

"He said that?" I sat forward and managed a weak grin. "He said that 'Dexter' part?"

She grabbed my toes through the blankets. "Would I pull your leg?"

"Believe you might try." I wiggled away.

At that point, feeling for the first time downright comfortable with her, I realized one more thing needed saying.

"Annabeth? Do you remember when you told me that maybe I knew more than I thought I did?"

"I believe so."

"Well, I believe you were right."

"Oh?" She scooted up and perched on the edge of the wooden stool. "What do you mean?"

I paused to sift my thoughts.

"My uncle once told me, 'Everybody's got a river inside.' And for the longest time, I studied and studied on that. And after a spell, I figured that river must be who we really are, our true spirit. Which, like any river, has got to run its own course."

I closed my eyes a moment. "Annabeth, on a map, which way does the Ohio flow through Crown Falls?"

"On a map? Well, I guess it'd be from east to west."

"But I'm asking, from which *side* to the other?"

She pursed her lips and puzzled a while. "Oh. You mean, from right to left?"

"From right to left," I said, nodding. "And do you suppose anyone would ever try and make it run the other way?"

She gave a small, knowing smile and shook her head. "I don't suppose anyone would."

"Me, neither," I said. "And that's what I saw on the riverbank while I was waiting for Pa. And now I see that trying to change someone's nature—the river inside—would be as bone-crazy as trying to turn around the great Ohio."

She leaned forward. "Luke, that is so—I mean, for you to see it in such a way." Her eyes darted over me. "You're a poet, aren't you? You are a natural poet."

I gave no answer. But I reckoned, by her standards, I probably was. And from her, that was high praise.

"Luke, promise me you'll send me a letter once you get settled up north. I know that boys don't like to write, but—"

"Annabeth." I stopped her. "You saved my life. I think I might do just about anything you asked."

A sparkle skipped through her eyes. "Then you will? You'll write and tell me everything you see and do?"

I nodded my head, blinking hard. "Shoot, I'll write you a hundred letters." And I tried to laugh. "Don't you remember? I'm different."

She beamed like the light through the blind. "You are," she said. "You truly are."

I had to lower my gaze from hers.

She leaned back in a stretch that bent her arms like wings. "Well," she said. "Suppose I'd best be getting on home."

She rose. I saw the weary resettle into her face.

"I know," she said, "that you all've got plenty church folk dropping by. But you let me know if—"

I nodded. "We will. We're much obliged."

She stood a while longer, smoothing her hands down her dress, as if taking measure of a thought. When she glanced back at me, her eyes had regained their gleam.

"Luke," she said, "your ma's a strong woman. I believe she'll be fine. And that little sister of yours—oh, she dropped straight from heaven."

"I know," I said. "Too bad she had to land on her head."

Annabeth laughed, and it felt so good to hear it.

"You are different, Luke Bledsoe." Then she stepped close, bent down, and kissed my cheek. "And don't you ever change that."

She squeezed my hand and left.

I sunk into my pillow, closing my eyes, memorizing the warmth and feel of her kiss.

I *was* different. And I was the same.

Time now, I figured, to let the river in me run its own true course.